APLEY TOWERS

Siren's Song

Myra King

D1332928

Sweet Cherry
Publishing

Sweet Cherry
Publishing

Published by Sweet Cherry Publishing Limited
Unit E, Vulcan Business Complex
Vulcan Road
Leicester, LE5 3EB
United Kingdom

www.sweetcherrypublishing.com

First published in the UK in 2015
ISBN: 978-1-78226-279-4

Illustrations © Creative Books
Illustrated by Subrata Mahajan
Cover design and illustration by Andrew Davis

Apley Towers: Siren's Song

Printed and bound by Thomson Press India Ltd.

For my father, Anthony King, who ditched work to see me get a Clear Round ribbon.

"All the world is made of faith, and trust, and pixie dust."
- J. M. Barrie

✥ One ✥

Beatrix King did not look happy. She sat atop her favourite Apley Towers horse, Slow-Moe, but there was no trace of her usual cheerful smile. And each unsuccessful attempt at dressage deepened the furrow in her forehead. Both horse and rider shook their heads in frustration as they trotted, once more, to the other end of the intermediate ring and began the dressage routine. Again.

Trixie looked, with jealousy, at the beginners' and advanced rings on either side of her. Why had she turned fourteen instead of staying at eight? Why could she not still have been at an easier level? Or why could her talent not lie with jumping? Why did it have to be complicated dressage that she happened to be good at? She looked down at the blonde girl in the ring directing her from the ground, and constantly on the move to avoid horse and rider.

"Angela, I think we have to accept the fact that I will

never be as good as you are. Or even half as good," she said with a shrug.

"Nonsense. Everything can be taught," Angela answered with her years of experience.

That blew Trixie's dressage-talent theory out of the window.

Angela May was extremely talented at dressage and had graciously agreed to teach Trixie all she knew. Trixie was an eager learner and talented in her own right but Slow-Moe was holding her back. As much as she hated to admit it, Trixie had outgrown the gelding.

"I'm going to start again."

"Take a walk around the ring to get your head right first."

On her way around, she spotted her other friend, Kaela Willoughby, duck into one of the stalls.

"Hope she's having a better time than I am," she said as she began the routine. Again.

Kaela had gotten bored of the dressage done badly and decided to walk around the stable. Technically March in South Africa was still summer, but it surely didn't feel that way. The sky was lost under a blanket of dark grey clouds and a cold wind blew across the feeding paddock and into the stables. It was the first time in over six months that Kaela had had to wear long sleeves.

Wendy Oberon, the stable owner, bustled past on her mobile talking about business problems Kaela hoped to never have.

Kaela walked around the stable to find something to do, but the three girls had already done the stable chores in order for Trixie to ride Slow-Moe. For the first time ever, there was nothing that needed to be done.

"Why are you wandering aimlessly around the stable?" a voice asked.

Kaela looked into the stall she had just passed. Bart, Wendy's son, had spoken to her. He had his own bay horse in a nursing stall and was running a wet soapy sponge over the brown coat. Mouse had his eyes closed in pleasure; Kaela was sure that the big horse was smiling.

"I'm bored," Kaela answered, "the dressage lesson is not going well and I really don't have the patience to watch the same routine done badly over and over again." She opened the stall door and went inside.

"Is the routine done badly because of the horse or the rider?" Bart asked. He had bent over the bucket of hot water to dip the sponge. He then squeezed the water out and dipped it again. Kaela's eyes fell on the muscles on his upper arm; they flexed and enlarged to twice their size when he squeezed. Kaela quickly looked at Mouse.

"Horse. Slow-Moe does not want to cooperate," Kaela said, picking up the steel comb at her feet.

She walked around Mouse and Bart to get to the bucket.

She knelt and dipped the comb in the warm soapy water. It felt good. The hot water warmed her numb fingers. She smiled as they began to tingle. Suddenly Bart dunked the sponge in the water, knocking the comb from Kaela's hand.

"Oh sorry, I didn't see you. You're lucky I didn't trip and land on you, my bum would have squashed you," Bart said.

"With those skinny cheeks? You must be kidding."

Bart turned on the spot, trying to get a good look at his backside. "They are not skinny. The gluteus maximus is maximusly gluteny."

"Whatever dude, stop spraying soapsuds everywhere."

He plunged his hands into the soapy water right along with hers. They crashed into each other and Kaela dropped the comb, again.

"First you threaten me with your butt, then you impede my help by making me drop the comb."

Bart smiled at her, retrieved the comb and held it out to her. It took her a moment to command her hand to reach up and take it. There was a long black streak that leaked from his pupil and into his iris like a wild mountain stream. It made her throat dry and her lungs stop.

"Thanks," she said softly.

Bart didn't seem to notice the odd static in the air; he went back to the conversation as though there hadn't been an interruption.

"It's not because Slow-Moe is not cooperating," he explained, "it's because Slow-Moe is not trained to do complicated dressage routines. He is a school horse – good at everything, *excellent* at nothing."

"That's harsh," Kaela said.

"It's the truth."

Kaela ran the warm, wet comb through Mouse's dark mane. The gelding's ears twitched and he sighed with pleasure.

"Have you heard about my mother's breeding plan?" Bart asked.

"Breeding plan?" *Does Wendy even have a boyfriend?*

"Yes, she wants to buy a stud," Bart said. He had moved around to Mouse's left side, he now stood right next to Kaela.

"She wants to buy instead of hire?" Kaela asked.

She knew Wendy wanted to breed with one of the stable mares, Honey. The mare was beautiful and Wendy was hoping it would be passed down. But buying a stud just for the hope of one good foal seemed like a waste of money.

"She wants to hire him out."

"Ah, she wants to make a profit on a horse, does she?" Kaela said in her best salesman tone.

Bart laughed and looked at Kaela; his blue eyes were twinkling, his dimple was showing, "She's trying to."

Kaela's wet fingers were starting to get cold, she didn't want to rub them on her clothes as she wasn't sure when the clothes would dry. She dunked the comb in the hot water again and began working on Mouse's tail. By the time she was finished with the tail, Bart had finished with Mouse's

10

bath. He picked up a baby-blue towel that had 'Mouse' embroidered on it in black thread and began drying the horse. Kaela moved out of his path and dropped the comb in the black bag that held Bart's grooming equipment. When she turned around, Bart stood facing her.

"Put your hands out," he said.

She did and he wrapped them in a green towel he was holding. He dried them and then let go, Kaela reluctantly took her hands back. She stared at her dry hands, slightly elevated, slightly disappointed. When she looked up, she met Bart's ice-blue eyes. He stared at her for a while, he looked on the verge of saying something – his lips parted several times but nothing came out. Finally he looked down and said, "Thanks for the help."

"You're welcome," she said.

It wasn't a wild mountain stream after all, it was a little creek in the forest: impossible to get to and only the rain could make it rise.

❦ Two ❧

Kaela followed her friends' voices through the stable. She found them outside of Slow-Moe's stall, they had the horse on cross ties and were both grooming him.

"Maybe we should put you on Fergie and see just how far along you are. Then we'll find a horse who is at that level," Angela said.

Fergie was Angela's Thoroughbred.

Trixie sighed, "I think that would be great, thanks for the offer." She didn't look happy though.

"How about we go saddle Fergie in the meantime?" Kaela said.

"Okay," Trixie said without even looking at her.

Angela and Kaela walked off to Fergie's stable.

"She's so sad," Angela said, linking her arm through Kaela's.

"Well, it's probably like losing a friend."

"She can still ride him, she just needs a trained dressage horse if she wants to compete," Angela said.

The girls came up to the stable, Fergie had her head out of the stall and was gazing longingly at the hills behind the paddocks.

"I promised you a ride in the Midlands when I could take you," Angela said to Fergie. "Don't make me feel more guilty than I already do."

"Where's Dawn?"

Angela's other horse, Dawn, lived in the stall next to Fergie. But the horse was nowhere to be seen.

"She's out in the paddock. I went to fetch Fergie when Trixie was on her outride," Angela said.

Kaela walked off to the tack room to fetch Fergie's tack while Angela quickly ran a dandy brush through her chestnut coat.

Trixie looked down at Slow-Moe's velvet nose. She couldn't believe that her time on the beautiful horse was over, it seemed like it had only just began.

Hot tears stung Trixie's eyes, she breathed deeply and blinked them back. She had come to love this horse as her own, and now she had to move on. She felt like she had to leave a bit of her own heart behind.

"Sometimes we have to accept that certain things were never meant to be part of our future," Joseph, a groom, said as he brought fresh hay for the horses. "Sometimes we have to leave things behind because they were never meant to come with us."

Trixie buried her head in Slow-Moe's mane. Why did Joseph always know what was going on in her heart?

As she breathed in the scents of her childhood, Trixie thought of the first time she had ridden Slow-Moe. She had been ten, had never ridden such a tall horse, and was absolutely terrified. He had ignored her command to canter, had tossed his head making her lose her reins, and had swivelled on the spot. She had flown off and landed beneath him. She had screamed at the view of his hooves on either side of her head but Slow-Moe had merely looked at her. From her upside-down perspective he appeared to be smiling. He had waited patiently for her to get out from beneath him and had only moved his hooves once she was at a safe distance. She had known then that Slow-Moe was made of something else. Slow-Moe would keep her safe no matter what. And he had since. Sure, there had been falls and bad days, but Slow-Moe had protected her just as she had protected him. He now looked for her when she was within earshot and worried about her when she lay on the ground after a fall. He was patient with her when she was learning dressage, and kept her from being bored when classes were dedicated only to jumping. How was she expected to walk away as though none of it had happened?

She ran her fingers over his neck and under his mane,

along his back and down his tail. Committing everything to memory. She didn't need to. Every part of him was etched in every fingerprint.

He may have never been hers in name, but he would always be hers in spirit.

"Maybe you should ride Toby," Kaela suggested as the three groomed Fergie. "He knows dressage."

"Toby is a bit too big for her," Angela added.

"Quiet Fire is far too big for me," Kaela defended.

"Yes but Quiet Fire is gentle, Toby is not."

"I'll ask Wendy if I can ride Toby in class tomorrow," Trixie said sadly.

She was not really listening though. She was comparing. Fergie had been an amazing mount, but she was no Slow-Moe.

There was a belief that mares were more spirited than geldings, and so they made the ride more of a challenge. At this point in life, Trixie knew she needed less of a challenge. She needed a horse that would understand that he could not move his hooves until she was at a safe distance. She didn't need a horse testing her riding abilities. Wendy did enough of that.

"Why is it that for every one hour you spend in the saddle, you have to spend two hours working around the stable?" Kaela asked.

"Because we are responsible horsewomen," Angela said quite seriously.

Kaela looked over at her concentration-creased face and laughed, "Ang, I was joking."

"Oh, sorry."

Because horses have discovered ways to make us their servants, Trixie thought.

But she didn't smile. There was no reason to smile.

Kaela frowned at the status.

> **PWF:** *Two years! We'll have it in two years. My heart is broken. But we will get it in two years!*

All the comments were in the Cree language. Phoenix, her mother and six brothers were Native Canadians who lived on the Cree reservation. Kaela had met Phoenix through LetsChat and the two, as well as Angela and Trixie, were part of a club called The Lost Kodas. A club sworn to be there whenever a member needed help.

Kaela quickly found Phoenix on her Chat list and typed a message.

> **Kaela:** What's happened?

Phoenix: My grandfather lost the election.

Kaela's heart thumped down into her stomach. The White Feather family had needed a break, and now they had lost it.

Kaela: I'm sorry. Does he know why he lost?

Phoenix: Too young.

Kaela: Your grandfather is too young?

Phoenix: He is twenty years younger than the other person running.

Kaela: Wisdom does not come with age.

Phoenix: Tell the voters that.

Kaela: That sucks, Phoenix. I'm so sorry. Don't let it get you down.

Phoenix: It's my grandfather I'm worried about. I don't want him to loose heart and never run again.

Kaela: Well if he's anything like the other White Feathers, I doubt he will give up without a fight!

❦ Three ❧

Angela was the only one of the three girls who did not live in Port St. Christopher. Her house – once home of South Africa's sugar baron, Lord Benedict Theodesius Sabian, an ancestor and creator of South Africa's largest sugar company – was in the neighbouring town of La Lucia. The same town also housed Trixie's grandmother. In fact, the two houses were on either end of a massive sugar field – the same sugar field Lord Sabian had bought over three hundred years ago and had used to begin his empire. That empire now dominated the sugar shelves in supermarkets and sat in nearly every cup of tea in South Africa and the neighbouring countries. It gave Angela goosebumps to look out at it and think that his legacy – his company and sugar fields – had, after three hundred years, only one heir left.

Angela.

Trixie had dognapped her grandmother's basset hound,

and had joined Angela in the field on the Sunday after the disastrous dressage lesson.

"No riding today?" she asked as she caught up with Angela.

The blonde rider shook her head, "The girls have the day off on Sunday."

Trixie looked at the never-ending sea of sugarcane, "My sister and I used to steal stalks when we were little. I wonder who we were stealing from."

Angela didn't dare tell her who owned the field.

"So, what are you going to do tomorrow?" she asked to change the subject.

Trixie shrugged and tugged on the leash, "I'll ask Wendy if I can ride Toby but I doubt she will let me. I've never seen Toby ridden by anyone but the best riders."

"Do you think maybe that's a sign that you need to look somewhere else for a rideable horse? I rode in the advanced class on Friday—"

"Why?" Trixie interrupted.

Angela shrugged, "I like to be part of something, instead of being the only one in my lesson."

"Good thinking."

"Anyway, I got to see all the horses. There are a few that may work. There is DeBurgh. I think he may be the next step up. Or Eagle and Honey."

"All Thoroughbreds."

"What's wrong with Thoroughbreds?" Angela asked in surprise.

Trixie shook her head as the two began walking uphill, "Absolutely nothing. Thoroughbreds are among the most prized horses in the world. But since they are hot-blooded, are they really the best dressage horses?"

Angela shrugged, "I suppose that all depends on the horse. Some humans can do things that others can't, but we don't blame it on our breed."

The girls were quiet as they climbed. When they finally reached the top of the hill, they took a minute to take it all in. The ocean, the sugarcane, the houses and, far in the distance, the Drakensburg Mountains. Angela got bored first. She had, of course, been staring at it her whole life. Her home caught her eye. She had left her curtains closed, which meant no sunlight had seeped in and warmed the place. She would have to get out of that habit before winter.

The basset howled as a colony of meerkats sauntered past, but he didn't bother getting up.

"Boog, you are so lazy," Trixie said with a shake of her head. "How did you find Fergie? When people go looking for dressage horses, they don't usually start with Thoroughbreds do they?"

Angela smiled at the memory, "We weren't looking for a dressage horse. We were looking for a jumper, and you can't deny that Thoroughbreds make the best jumpers."

"Not at all."

"I wanted to go to Tumbledowns to look for one. You know Tumbledowns, the Thoroughbred breeders in the Midlands?"

Trixie nodded.

"I wanted one from them and I kept begging my dad to take me, and he just kept putting it off. But I just knew my perfect horse was there. It was like a siren's song, you know those old stories about the women who lived in the sea and sang to sailors to lure them over? It was like that. I could hear it in my head. I knew the perfect horse was there and it was singing to me."

"So what happened?"

"*Months* went by and my father still didn't take me. Then one morning, Dad came down the stairs with this *wild* look in his eye. He didn't even say good morning, he didn't say anything. He just grabbed his car keys and told me to come. We drove out to the Midlands and as we were pulling into Tumbledowns, a horsebox pulled in too. And I just knew that my horse was in that horsebox."

"And was she?"

"Yes!" Angela cried excitedly. "As soon as she stepped off the trailer and looked at me, the wind was blowing through her mane and the sun was shining down on her. And I just knew she was the one I had been searching for. And I also knew that her name had something to do with the wind. And I don't know how I knew that, I just did."

"But her name is Fergie."

Angela shook her head, "That's her nickname because of the colour of her hair. Her real name is Summer Breeze. And somehow I just knew it."

Trixie looked at her with unveiled amazement. Boog howled as more meerkats ran past.

"So what happened? How did you go from searching for a jumper, to using her as a dressage horse?"

"We spoke to the owner, it turned out that she had just come off the racetrack. They were bringing her back that morning because she kept losing at the races and they'd sold her back to Tumbledowns."

"So, if you had gone before that day you wouldn't have found her?"

"Exactly," Angela said in wonder, "it was like it was meant to be."

Trixie nodded, "So what happened?"

"She wasn't winning because she never wanted to go fast. She can, when the mood takes her – that woman could give the speed of sound a run for its money. But she never *wanted* to. They tacked her up for me, and I didn't even bother jumping. I just tested her with a simple dressage routine, something even beginners can do. She was perfect. And that is how I knew I had found my dressage horse. I just knew. She sang to me and I found her."

Wind rippled through the sugarcane, making it dance with the earth in waves that dipped and rose like music.

"But that is for buying a horse," Trixie finally said, "you knew it was the right horse to *buy*. I'm just looking for one to ride."

"I think it is the same principal, just on a limited scale.

Do you feel that Toby is the horse you'll be riding for the next few years?"

"Not at all."

"Well then you'll be open to riding different horses this week."

Trixie nodded and looked back at the cane.

Angela heard a slight *hiss* and looked up into the only tree on the hill. A long, fat green snake stared back at her. It was only a Natal green snake; they were harmless but sometimes inexplicably fell off branches and onto the people walking beneath. Nearly fifteen kilograms of snake suddenly landing on your shoulders is enough to make the most hardened man cry. Angela moved over to Trixie and Boog.

"Do you think we could steal a stalk?" Trixie said. "Do you think the owner would mind if we took just one?"

Angela shook her head, "No, the owner won't mind."

She wasn't the owner, but she knew her father wouldn't mind.

Between the two girls, they huffed and puffed and pulled a stalk out. They then split it open, and pulled off pieces of pure sugar with their teeth.

Sweetness exploded throughout Angela's mouth. She laughed as Trixie put the stalk to her mouth, gripped it with her teeth, scrunched her nose and ripped a large piece off.

Angela had never taken the sugarcane straight from the field and eaten it. She had never taken any notice of this crop. It had simply been something her ancestor had insisted on growing and had made a fortune on. But it had never been part of who she was. Or at least, it had never been the part of her life that she found important. She bit into the stalk and ripped more sugar off. More sweetness spread across her tongue. She stared out at the vast universe of sugarcane as it danced in the wind.

"Wanna know a secret?"

Trixie nodded and ripped more sugar.

"One day, I will own all of this."

"I'm not sure that's a good idea," Wendy said wearily.

It was Monday afternoon and Trixie had just asked if she could ride Toby in her lesson.

"Why not?" Trixie asked.

"Well, Toby is an advanced horse: he might be a bit difficult for you. He is used to riders who make very few, if any, mistakes. He might react badly to an intermediate rider," Wendy explained.

"Well, if it doesn't go well we can forget the whole thing?" Trixie asked sweetly. "I have to try, at least."

Wendy bit her bottom lip and raised her eyebrows, she looked out at the paddock, looking for Toby. She tilted her head one way and then the next. Finally she turned to Trixie.

"No, Toby is too …" she shook her head. "If you want to move up in dressage we can start you on DeBurgh."

Relief flooded over Trixie like an ocean wave, "Okay, I'll ride him then."

She raced off before Wendy had a chance to change her mind.

"Hey, where are you off too?" Russell cried as she zoomed past.

Trixie rolled her eyes.

Why can't Russell get a girlfriend and leave me alone? she wondered.

"I need to tack DeBurgh."

"DeBurgh? What about Slow-Moe?"

The pain ripped through Trixie like a whip from an aggravated horse's tail. She had put the loss of Slow-Moe out of her mind until that point. She stopped running and struggled to breathe.

He is still in the field, she thought, *I can go get him right now. I can ride him instead.*

Hot tears burned her eyes and she struggled to blink them back.

She had lost a friend.

She remembered a particular sunny spring morning where she had lain in the feeding paddock and stared at the endless blue sky. Slow-Moe, in his usual dawdle, had ambled over and spent the rest of the afternoon grazing near her. The quiet solitude of horse and rider, taken away from everything that distracted her from the simple truth of existence, had burned into Trixie's soul. It meant that she came back to that place whenever it all became too much.

And now, she came back alone.

"Are you okay?" Russell asked.

He had sneaked up to her, and just this once, she didn't mind.

"I think I have changed my mind."

"About?"

"About riding DeBurgh, or anyone. I want Slow-Moe."

"You want me to get him?"

And that broke the enchantment. Russell, kind-hearted and exhausting Russell, offering to get Slow-Moe meant that Trixie would always be stuck where she was. She would never progress; never leave this quaint little world she had made.

She had to be brave and move on.

"No, no, it's okay. I need to ride DeBurgh. I'll get him."

She left Russell standing in the corridor and went to get DeBurgh.

She would move forward.

Even if it broke her heart.

"I told you."

"No, no, no, you told me that your father was a farmer."

"He is."

"You didn't tell me he was *the* farmer."

"Oh Kaela, what does it matter?"

27

"Do you know the history of your family?"

Angela sighed, "No, but I'm assuming you are going to tell me."

"*Major* conservation. And I mean *major*. Entire parts of the Natal forests and beaches have been saved by your ancestors. My own grandfather even bought a bit of land off your ancestor. Land he had rescued from developers and kept as farmland."

"Really?" Angela asked excitedly.

"Yes, it's now part of our farm in the Midlands."

"So our ancestors knew each other?" Angela asked. "So we were destined to meet."

Kaela smiled, "Oh, I *love* destiny. Imagine all the other things that are destiny."

"Getting tired of my life at my last stable and coming here instead and meeting you and becoming a koda," Angela said with a smile.

"You see ... how awesome is destiny?" Kaela said dramatically. "What you need is handed to you when you need it."

"What you are seeking seeks you?"

"But of course."

Kaela laughed at Angela and went back to tacking Quiet Fire. Finding out that her newfound friend was a descendant of Lord Sabian had been the highlight of her weekend. She didn't particularly find the Lord himself anything impressive – but his descendants had done amazing things for South

Africa. Half of the National Parks and the majority of the Midlands could thank the Sabian family for their existence. The Midlands were the lands surrounding the Drakensburg Mountains, they were mostly useless as farming lands but they were bought out by the Sabians and sold off as smaller properties. It was now a horse-lover's paradise: breeding farms of all kinds as well as adventure ranches and, of course, Equestrian International – the illustrious riding academy – were all in the Midlands. There was also a racetrack, which hosted South Africa's Spectacle of Kings – an illustrious race where the wealthiest riders and owners could show off their best racing horses.

And it was all thanks to the Sabian family.

"Angela! Don't you realise how awesome this all is?" she cried again.

"No, but I'm assuming you won't stop telling me until you get bored."

"Well, until I find someone else with impressive ancestors."

Trixie sighed for the tenth time. The lesson was not going well.

It didn't help that for some unknown reason there was bluegrass music playing across the riding ring.

"I feel like I am in New Orleans," Kaela cried.

The banjo and harmonica accompanied a sorrowful voice like a mouth devoid of teeth. Trixie could imagine a man wearing blue dungarees and singing about the harvest moon while a bloodhound howled next to him.

It would've been a pretty picture, but not when she was trying to concentrate on her riding.

"Is Bart feeling okay?" Russell asked, looking from the house and then towards their teacher.

Wendy shrugged.

DeBurgh, trotting along with no care in the world, seemed bored with the lesson. He was, of course, trained for more than this. Although, Trixie couldn't help but think he could at least show some interest.

"Shall we jump?" Wendy said.

"Yes please," Kaela piped.

Trixie rolled her eyes, she couldn't wait for her own private dressage lesson tomorrow where she would not have to worry about the silly necessity of having to stay on the horse while it acted like a rabbit.

Wendy set the jump up, it was only two feet which made it half a foot less than they were used to jumping at.

Which meant it was so low for Trixie's benefit.

At that point, she almost stood in her stirrups and told Wendy, under no uncertain terms, that she didn't care about jumping so she might as well jack that jump up to its highest height. Trixie then imagined herself simply walking away.

If only.

"Okay, jump."

Kaela was the first to go. She, as always, soared without a problem. She made it look as though there was no skill involved. Bella was next. Along with Kaela, she looked like a pro. Although Trixie had to admit, Kaela shone more. Bella sneered as she approached the jump and scorned as she went over. Kaela knew she was on show. She approached as a queen would, and flew as though she was on the back of a dragon. Everyone watched her, no one bothered with Bella.

The rest of the class went after, they all did well.

Then it was Trixie's turn. She faced DeBurgh to the jump and nudged him forward. He cantered towards the jump and turned sideways at the last moment. Bella snorted.

Trixie whipped the horse around and trotted him back to the fence.

"You *will* do this you grumpy old man," she hissed.

He whipped her with his tail.

She kicked him into a canter, he raced forward and stopped instead of lifting.

Trixie looked at Wendy, "And I'm done."

Kaela was extremely curious about the music.

When the rest of the class returned their horses to the stalls, Kaela turned Quiet Fire in the opposite direction. She walked him along the car park and passed the house. The bluegrass music blared from outside speakers.

Some sorrow-tortured son of the south sang about his love being his sunshine. Kaela nudged Quiet Fire into a slow walk along the wall. Beyond the music she could hear small splashes.

Bart must be in the pool.

She sat taller in the saddle until she could see over the stone wall surrounding the pool area. There was Bart, in green goggles and a black swimming cap, racing across the pool at speeds Kaela could only achieve on horseback. She pulled Quiet Fire to a halt and leaned against the wall, her chin supported by her crossed arms.

She counted as Bart did twenty laps in the time it would take everyone else to do four. Finally, he stopped and leaned against the side of the pool in much the same way Kaela was positioned. He took huge gulps of air and then turned his head to face her. She smiled at him and he smiled at her.

"You are a merman."

He laughed at that, "I wouldn't go that far."

"What's with the music?"

"I'm hoping to out-swim it."

There was some logic in that somewhere.

She picked up Quiet Fire's reins and turned him around, "I'll see you later Neptune."

Bart pushed himself away from the wall and waved. He did a backwards dive and continued swimming.

Kaela smiled at the view.

"So it just wasn't good?"

Trixie shook her head.

"Ang, am I being a fool?"

"Of course not," Angela frowned. "Why would you say that?"

"Because I'm throwing away a good horse to ride one that is bored with doing what horses do."

Angela shrugged and went back to grooming DeBurgh, "What do you feel?"

"I don't."

Angela had no idea what advice to give. For her, riding was a challenge. DeBurgh would be seen as an adventure. She was starting to believe that Trixie was expecting it to be too easy. She wanted a push-button horse, but unless she suddenly won more than a million in the lottery, she would not get one. Push-button horses were expensive because you bought them already trained.

"Next stop is Eagle," she finally said.

"I suppose." Trixie said with no enthusiasm.

She gathered DeBurgh's tack and took it back to where it belonged.

Angela gave the chestnut Thoroughbred a good pat on the neck and a cheeky tickle under the mane, then left the stall. Her mother would be here soon, and she would have to wait for her in the car park.

After she had said bye to everyone she made her way to her usual spot under the oak tree to wait. Jeremy, the stable donkey, came over to search for snacks but there were none. He quickly left.

Bart came around the corner and smiled when he saw her, Angela quickly looked around hoping Kaela was nowhere to be seen. Bart was severely off-limits to everyone.

"Hi Ang, can I ask you a question?"

Make it quick buddy, "Sure, of course."

"How are the competitions at Equestrian International? Are they harder than everywhere else?"

Angela could only hope that Kaela had not seen her spending nearly fifteen minutes explaining the academy competitions.

Or Bart, staring so intently as she spoke.

❦ Four ❧

Amy, one of the beginner riders, had been left in the care of Kaela's family as her parents had gone out of the country on business. Unlike Kaela, she had no interest in spending all afternoon at the stable and the two girls left shortly after the lessons ended. The short walk back to the Willoughby house was punctuated by Amy and her discussions on anything her eyes happened to land on. Before they had even reached the gate and gotten onto the property, Amy had probably spoken more than Kaela had planned to for the next ten years.

She kept her chatter up all the way across the garden, through the house (stopping only to say hello to Kaela's grandmother and to talk her ear off a bit too), up the stairs and into Kaela's room. And then the running commentary on the bedroom décor began.

Kaela had to lie on the bed to recoup lost energy. She

wondered just how this child could talk so much. How had she not run out of things to say?

Kaela stared at the posters on her ceiling. Her favourite band, Jamiroquai, spread in never-ending wallpaper across her line of sight. In an attempt to block out Amy's commentary, she studied the posters. Most of them had the lead singer wearing his infamous Native American-style headdress. This just reminded Kaela of Phoenix and the rest of the White Feather family. Kaela hadn't heard from Phoenix, nor had she put any statuses up. Kaela rolled on her side and stared out of her balcony doors, she could only hope that the family weren't taking the election loss too badly.

She sighed and brought her attention back to Amy. The girl still chattered away. Inspired, apparently, by the books on Kaela's shelf.

"Why are there no superheroes who are girls?" Amy piped up.

Kaela shrugged, she hated superhero stories so she couldn't care less if there were none. In fact, she did know of some, but she wasn't really in the mood to give Amy a quick lesson in females with superpowers.

"There should be more superhero stories with girls being superheroes."

"So write them."

Finally, Amy was silenced. She stared at Kaela in wonder and, maybe, realisation of what she could achieve.

Kaela took the hiatus as opportunity to switch her stereo on. Hopefully Jamiroquai would keep Amy from starting up again.

Wrong.

"Oh I love Jamiroquai. My mom plays their music all the time. I can sing all the words. Let me show you."

Kaela quickly escaped to her balcony. Once there, she gave a quick glance at her bedroom. A mattress had been put down for Amy. This left very little space for movement – you could either stand on the bed, the mattress or the desk. The claustrophobia was likely to send her more crazy than Amy's constant talking would. It was at moments like these that Kaela appreciated her balcony. Her room was the only upstairs bedroom; it had once been her mother's art studio, but with her mother gone, Kaela had simply adopted the room as her own. She had a tiny little balcony that overlooked the pool and trampoline area. Although it was nearing dark and she could hear the table being set for dinner, she was glad to get out of the suffocation of her room and breathe the fresh air. She had no intention of leaving her nice, open balcony. She watched the sun set over the mountains and thought about Phoenix.

The dogs ran into the pool area and began barking wildly. Kaela watched them in annoyance. Why were they disturbing her peace?

"What are you mutts barking at?"

The huskies only barked louder.

"You are ruining my chi!"

They began to howl.

Kaela groaned and turned away from the furry noise-makers. She found herself looking into the staring face of a vervet monkey who had made himself at home on the banister next to her.

Kaela screamed and ran back into her room. The monkey screamed and jumped into the tree. Five other monkeys jumped from the roof to the railing to the tree.

"What's all the noise about?" Alice, her grandmother, asked.

"Monkeys!" Kaela screamed.

"Hide the soap!"

"I have lots of monkey stories," Amy said excitedly.

From: trixie-true@feaguemail.co.za
To: kaelalw2000@feaguemail.co.za; phoenix-wfeather@feaguemail.com; horsecrazyang@feaguemail.co.za
Subject: Horse Trial #1

Good evening kodas,
As you all know my hunt for a new dressage horse began today. I cannot say it went well. I'm not one for blaming the horse (a carpenter never blames

his tools, after all) but today I blame the horse.

REASONS FOR BLAMING THE HORSE
1) The horse was the one who did not jump.
2) The horse was the one who spent the entire lesson being bored.
3) The horse kept ignoring my directions.
4) The horse was not Slow-Moe.

I have spoken to each of you and have collected your theories.

THEORIES FROM THE LOST KODAS
Angela: I did not want to jump, why should the horse bother jumping?
Kaela: I am expecting too much from one lesson: my first lesson with Slow-Moe did not go well either ("In fact, if I am to trust my memories, it went worse" – Kaela said that, not me).
Phoenix: I was disappointed that DeBurgh was not Slow-Moe, DeBurgh was disappointed he was not grazing in the field. It was a recipe for disaster.

SCIENCE EXPERIMENT CONCLUSION BASED ON EVIDENCE PRESENTED
The kodas blame me and not the horse.

TOMORROW'S EXPERIMENT

Ride Eagle and hope it goes better. Wendy has suspended the private lessons until I find a new horse. So I'll be riding in the main class.

P.S. I miss Slow-Moe.

Trixie clicked 'send' and slumped back onto her bed. This was harder than any other science experiment she'd ever had to do.

"Angela May! To what do I owe the honour?"

Angela smiled at her father as she walked towards him.

"I just thought I would walk the sugarcane field with you."

The dogs ran up, circled her and dashed off into the sugarcane.

"Copernicus … Tesla … Get back here," George May cried.

The dogs raced back to the path and circled their owners again.

"Don't you find it odd that there is only you left?" Angela asked.

"Me left? Who's gone?"

"I mean, Lord Sabian had like forty children and you are all that's left of that huge family."

"He had ten children. And between me and him there have been a lot of wars. And then the descendants just kept having only one child. And now here we are. All that's left."

"So if you think it's bad to have only one child, why didn't you have more? Why just me?"

George sighed and yelled at the dogs again, then he said, "It was hard enough getting you."

Angela had always found it odd how her parents always said 'getting you' instead of 'having you'. But she said nothing and continued to walk through the fields with her father.

"Have you ever pulled a stalk and eaten it?" she asked.

George shook his head, "Not since I was a little kid."

Angela rushed forward, pushed Copernicus and Tesla out of the way, and grabbed a stalk. She ripped it out and began tearing it with her teeth.

George laughed at her, "It is a good thing I'm not sending you to finishing school, they'd kick you right back out."

Angela chewed on the sugary strings and handed the stalk to her father. He laughed again and took it. He ripped it with his teeth just as his daughter had.

"I still prefer the sugar in my tea," he said.

"Yeah, but this way is fun too."

"Maybe this is why all our ancestors only had one kid: too many kids would rip the sugarcane fields to pieces."

⨪ Five ⨪

Trixie looked up at Eagle. He was beautiful in his tack. She had never ridden him before and the way he was pacing from side to side gave her slight apprehension. Still, nothing ventured, nothing gained.

"Riding Eagle today?"

Trixie rolled her eyes. When was Russell going to get a girlfriend and leave her alone?

"Yes, I need to find a new dressage horse."

"So you are riding Eagle?" he asked with a frown and leaned against the stall door.

No, I've tacked him up for the fun of it. I am actually planning on sitting this class out, she thought with frustration.

"Yes. I am riding him today."

"But is he really the best horse for dressage?"

"I don't know, I haven't ridden him yet," she said with a bit too much bite.

He looked at her but didn't say anything. His stare made her nervous.

"Good luck with the ride."

And then he walked off.

Great, Trixie thought, *now I have made an enemy out of Russell.*

"Riders, where are you?" Wendy cried.

Trixie grabbed her hard hat and led Eagle out of the stall. She watched the way he moved and how he stopped. He held himself as a dressage horse should. That was a good sign.

She quickly adjusted her stirrup leathers and mounted.

Bella, Russell and Kaela were already warming their horses up in the intermediate ring. Trixie waited for the equine train to pass and joined at the back, right behind Russell and Vanity Fair. Eagle automatically put his ears back.

That was not a good sign.

Once the entire class had trotted in their endless circles around the ring, Wendy began the lesson. Easy stuff at first, but progressively harder as the hour wore on. Twice Trixie had had to pull Eagle back into line. Twice more he had bolted off with her. She whipped him around and got him back in line.

"Trix, put him in front, maybe that will make him happy."

Trixie, at the back of the parade, slowed Eagle down so that he would then take the lead. He did this without a problem until he realised the widening gap between him and Vanity Fair was only getting bigger. He tossed his head against the bit and cantered towards the dappled grey. Vanity gave a small buck and Eagle had to turn to avoid her hooves.

Trixie had had to grab the pommel to keep from falling, but Russell's legs held him as though the horse beneath him had not even moved, let alone bucked her back legs to an impressive height.

"I tried to tell you … That horse will never be a dressage horse. He is made for speed," he said.

Trixie scowled at him.

"Don't give me that look just because I'm right."

"Don't be a jerk just because you're right!" she screamed at him.

Wendy clapped her hands, "Okay, everybody head out to the feeding paddock and gallop across it. You all need to feel the wind in your hair."

"We've got hard hats on," Kaela reminded her.

"Fine, you all need to feel wind in your eyeballs," she corrected and held the gate open.

Russell and Bella walked out first, the two kept their horses next to each other until they were in the feeding paddock. Trixie stared at the two of them in anger.

"I don't think they are gossiping about you, if that makes you feel any better," Kaela said as she pulled Quiet Fire next to Eagle, who automatically put his ears down and stomped. "And you … behave!"

Eagle ignored her.

"How do you know they aren't gossiping about me?"

"Firstly, what do you care? Secondly, Russell is better than that."

"So why did he explode on me?"

"You probably hurt him at the stalls, when he was just trying to help you."

"He was bugging me."

"It is not his fault he likes you, be grateful someone does."

Trixie stared at Kaela in shock, did she detect a hint of insult in that statement? But then she remembered Kaela, and her brutal honesty, and knew she was probably right anyway.

"Sorry to interrupt guys."

The girls turned to look at Emily, another intermediate rider.

"Trix, I've been trying to decide where I want to go with riding, and dressage is at the bottom of the list. Casino is pretty well trained in dressage and the two of us are clashing. I want to race and jump to the stars and he wants to dance on the spot. So how would you feel about us swapping for tomorrow's lesson? You take Casino and I take Eagle?"

"Gladly," Trixie said without a thought.

When the riders reached the brick wall on the far end of the paddock, they all turned their horses to face Wendy who gave them the signal to gallop.

None of them did.

"Shall we race?" Bella asked.

"You only want to race because your horse is off the racetrack," Jasmyn said.

"So is Eagle," Bella said, staring sharply at Trixie.

"Okay, before Wendy gives herself a heart attack, let's race," Russell said.

"On your marks, get set …" Emily started.

"Go!" they all screamed and kicked their horses into action.

Quiet Fire gained ground first, as always, and Kaela was almost a full horse in front.

Eagle, finally able to do what he loved, powered under as much rein as Trixie could give him. KaPoe and Bella kept time with them. The two Thoroughbreds were nose to nose. Trixie looked over at Bella and kicked Eagle again, the horse shot further ahead but was quickly caught up by Russell. She looked over at him. There was determination in his eyes, as though he was thinking that if he could beat her, she couldn't hurt him any more. Trixie pulled slightly on the reins to slow Eagle down. Vanity Fair overtook and caught up with Kaela and Quiet Fire. The race was theirs. Trixie watched as the two reached the wooden fence together. Russell reined Vanity in but Kaela, ever the competitive one, jumped the fence.

Eagle seemed happier, Trixie let herself relax and got into his steady rhythm. She had no rules or expectations or demands. She just was.

Sometimes she forgot that this was what riding was all about ... Being free.

Kaela: Are you okay? Haven't heard from you in a while.

Phoenix: Just sad for my grandfather. He has gone to the sweat lodge.

Kaela: Is that Native American for saying he has gone insane?

Phoenix: HAHA! NO! A sweat lodge is a sacred room to go to fast and pray and try to find answers. Like a synagogue or church, or a mosque. He and Chiron have gone. It's Chiron's first time. If he has a vision then he will have a tribal name based on that vision.

Kaela: But I like his name! Here's hoping he has a vision of a planet.

Phoenix: He will still be named Chiron. He will just have a tribal name as well.

Kaela: Like Dancing with a Wolf?

Phoenix: I hope not.

Kaela: My mother loved that movie. It was one of the last she ever watched. Did you know that the tribe in the movie are the Lakota?

Phoenix: They are our neighbouring tribe. So is that why your dog is named after the Lakota? Because of your mother?

Kaela closed her eyes. Why had she started this?

Kaela: I suppose.

Phoenix: My father named my horse. Wind Whistler. When he was at the sweat lodge he said that the wind spoke to him, almost like it sang to him.

Kaela: What did it tell him?

Phoenix: "Honour the horse!"

Good advice.

From: trixie-true@feaguemail.co.za
To: kaelalw2000@feaguemail.co.za; phoenix-wfeather@feaguemail.com; horsecrazyang@feaguemail.co.za
Subject: Horse Trial #2

Good evening kodas,
Horse trial #2 was worse than horse trial #1.

REASONS IT WAS TERRIBLE
1) Horse young and energetic.
2) Horse not interested in dressage.
3) Horse has a crush on Vanity Fair.
4) I want to avoid Vanity Fair.
5) And her rider.
6) Horse not Slow-Moe.
7) I hurt a friend.

INFORMATION GATHERED FROM KODAS.
Angela: It can only get better from here.
Kaela: Why aren't you riding Slow-Moe? How much dressage time have you actually wasted on this wild goose chase? (She said that, not me.)
Phoenix: Maybe I need to consider training Slow-Moe.

CONCLUSION BASED ON EVIDENCE

The kodas believe I should return to Slow-Moe. Maybe I should.

TOMORROW'S EXPERIMENT
Riding Casino.

P.S. I miss Slow-Moe

⊱ Six ⊰

To keep Dawn interested in the working life, Angela sometimes rode her in the intermediate class with Trixie and Kaela.

Since Dawn and Casino were already tacked, the two riders left Kaela and made their way to the ring. She watched them leave with a sour lump in her throat and sore spot on her chest.

"What's up with you?" Bart asked as he walked past.

His hair was wet, yet he was still in his school uniform.

"Have you just got back from swimming practice?"

"Yes, I had to put a wet swimsuit on. I can't tell you how great that was," he said with a shudder.

"Why was it wet?"

"This morning the coach pulled me out of class to teach the young 'uns how to do butterfly stroke. Isn't that *his* job?"

"At least you got pulled out of class and your swimming got complimented."

"One day, Miss Willoughby, I will swim in the Empire Games."

"For which country?"

"Aaah, this one," he said with a frown.

"Are you allowed to swim for South Africa? You were born in England."

A dark cloud swept over his face then. It was obvious that Bart had never thought of this. He quickly replaced it with a smile, deepening his dimple for emphasis.

Kaela returned his smile, but she had to wonder if she had just dashed his dreams.

"Why were you looking so moody when I first walked up?"

Kaela put her head against a fully tacked Quiet Fire, "Angela is riding in our class."

"So?"

She shrugged, "It bugs me a little."

"Why?"

She quickly stuck her head out of the stall to make sure no one was around, "can I tell you a secret?"

"Do I have to tell you one?"

"No, you can just owe me."

"Okay tell me, I won't tell," Bart stuck his pinky out and Kaela locked it with hers.

"As much as I love Angela and I do, I am so jealous of her."

Kaela was inches away from Bart now, their heads leaned in close to whisper secrets.

"Why?"

"The fact that Angela has her own horse," Kaela shrugged.

"So does half the stable."

"And she is homeschooled so she can ride for six hours a day. And she is a *brilliant* rider. The best I have ever seen. And she is so far ahead that I know I will never catch up."

"What's this got to do with her riding in your class?"

"It is a fly in my ointment."

"You are in the right place for flies."

There were ten hovering around the two as they spoke.

"I'm serious!" Kaela said with a smile. "All the other riders look like novices compared to Angela. Not to mention that it also goes a bit deeper than that."

"How deep?"

"Deep. Today we are jumping, and in jumping Quiet Fire and I set the stage alight. We look so good together people might as well pay to see us."

"In your modest opinion," Bart joked.

"As long as Angela is in the ring, we will always be second best."

Kaela pulled away from Bart's ear and stared at him. His blue eyes flashed at her. He gave her a half-smile and raised one of his eyebrows, "But how wrong you are. You could never be second best at anything."

"With Angela and Dawn, yes I am."

Bart shrugged and pulled his finger back, "What does it

matter what you look like? As long as you are having fun and enjoying the lesson, who cares?"

Kaela shrugged, "it's important to me. I'm not the best student at school and I suck at dressage, so jumping is my talent."

"Someone will always be better than you at something," Joseph said as he untacked Sun Dancer in the opposite stall. "there will always be a bigger fish."

Kaela and Bart looked over at Joseph, neither had even known he was there.

"That thought sucks," Bart said.

Joseph chuckled and shrugged, "Acceptance has to come from within. If you are happy because of something that can be taken away from you, then you will never be happy."

Bart and Kaela looked at each other, something about that made perfect sense.

"Also, if you are any later for class, you will be seriously unhappy," Joseph added and gestured out towards Wendy, already stood in the ring and frowning.

Kaela quickly grabbed her hard hat and ran, horse trotting behind her, to the ring where the class were already mounted and walking around.

"Nice of you to join us, Kaela," Wendy said.

"So happy to be here!" she cried and got into line behind Russell.

The riders warmed up their horses by walking three circles, trotting three more and finally cantering the last three. Wendy had them go over trotting poles, which the class had not done for years.

"You have all forgotten what you are doing," Wendy said.

The only one getting it right besides Angela was, surprisingly, Trixie. She kept her perfect position as Casino rabbit-hopped over the poles. She didn't even appear to be trying.

Maybe she has found the perfect horse, Kaela thought.

Emily and Eagle zoomed over the trotting poles, knocking every one.

"Extend your trot," Wendy called.

"Isn't the horse supposed to do that on his own?" Emily called back.

Wendy shook her head, "Kaela, you're up."

Kaela trotted Quiet Fire in a circle and brought him up to the poles. She gave him the signals to extend his trot, he ignored them. He trotted his hooves too closely and knocked nearly every pole, even refusing to go over the last one. Kaela fell forward in the saddle at his sudden stop.

"Extend the trot," Wendy said.

"I told him to."

"Obviously not well enough. Russell, let's go."

Kaela trotted Quiet Fire out of the way and over to the fence. She was only half surprised to see Bart sitting on the top rung, she had, after all, been watching him a few days before. Quiet Fire went over to beg for treats.

"You are not listening, good Sir," Bart said as he stroked

Quiet Fire's velvet nose, "the lady is telling you what to do and you are ignoring her."

"Perhaps you need to give him some advice," Kaela suggested with a smile.

"Some advice, some advice," Bart said in a sing-song voice. "My mother always tells me that the way to a woman's heart is by knowing how to vacuum."

"Quiet Fire is already in my heart."

"Okay, that doesn't apply. How about this, maybe if the lady relaxed and felt confident it would all go well. Confidence is key."

Bart looked up at her. The sun shone directly in his eyes, making them sapphire pools.

"I *am* confident," she said.

"As you should be. Even though there are six other riders and horses in this ring, the only ones who shine are you two."

"We really shine?" Kaela asked with one eyebrow up.

"Yes, literally, the sun is shining on you."

"Oh, haha. You are so funny," she said with as much sarcasm as she could muster.

Bart smiled at her, reflecting the sunlight.

"Why are you watching?"

"A Siren lured me over."

"Kaela, stop gossiping and get that horse over these poles," Wendy cried.

As she turned Quiet Fire, Bart said, "Be confident, you are the best in the ring."

Be confident, you are the best in the ring.

"All right Quiet Fire, let's do this."

She closed her eyes and thought about herself on horseback. Deep down she knew there would always be someone better. There would always be a bigger fish. Nothing she did could do would ever change that. The only thing she could do was be confident in her own abilities. There was no one else in the world like her. There may be some better (and some worse), but only *she* could bring together her separate quirks and talents to make her ride *her* ride.

And that would always make her good enough.

She opened her eyes and smiled. This time, when she gave the signals, Quiet Fire listened. She made it across the poles without a hitch and joined Angela and Trixie on the other side.

"I am a Siren," she whispered.

"Please don't sing," Trixie said.

"Bart, make yourself useful and build me a jump."

"Yes, Mum. Anything else while I am at it? Cup of tea? Plate of biscuits? World peace?"

"No backchat."

The girls trotted their horses around the ring as Bart set the jump up. Trixie inexplicably changed diagonals and then changed them again. Kaela supposed she was putting Casino through the paces. She then let go of the reins and directed the horse with just her legs.

"Ang, do something dressagey so I can copy."

Angela pulled Dawn out of line and joined Trixie in the middle, the two put the horses through a simple dressage routine. This left Kaela trotting on her own. Bart smiled at her, she smiled back.

Be confident, you are the best in the ring.

She turned Quiet Fire and brought him in line with the jump.

"Are you going to move?" she asked Bart.

He shook his head and leaned on the jump, "I trust you."

"You trust me too much."

"Go on, I am confident you can do it."

"You are confident I can jump without killing you?"

Bart nodded.

He was far to the right of the jump. Quiet Fire wouldn't go anywhere near him.

Kaela smiled and nudged Quiet Fire who went into a canter towards the jump. Bart didn't move. He stared her right in the eye. And he was getting closer.

Three paces, two paces, one pace.

She flew.

"Bart! Stop being an idiot. Kaela, don't let him wrangle you into his idiotic, death-defying schemes," Wendy cried.

Kaela turned in the saddle, Bart still smiled at her, "See, I'm confident you are the best."

"I'm the best at jumping with you hanging onto the jump?"

Bart shrugged and walked over to Quiet Fire, he pulled

Kaela's foot out of the stirrup, put his own foot in and lifted himself up so that he stood, in mid-air, next to Kaela. He leaned into her ear and whispered, "did you happen to notice that no one in the ring was watching Angela when you jumped? All eyes were on you."

He slipped his foot out and jumped down.

"You set the stage alight."

The sound of the hoofbeats on the dirt floor echoed across the barren lands. Trixie always found it startling that land that was caught between ocean and mountain could be so flat. She liked astrophysics and not geology, but secretly she hoped that when she began to study the cosmos, someone would explain to her why her home was pancake-flat.

Russell rode next to her. He hadn't said a word since the day before.

"Hey Rusty," she said.

There was a ghost of a smile on his lips but he didn't turn around. Trixie was the only one to call him Rusty and she only did it because, on his tenth birthday, he had confessed how disappointed he was that his cake had said 'Happy Birthday Russ' instead of 'Rusty'. It had been her nickname for him since.

"I'm sorry about the way I behaved yesterday. I was being mean for no reason."

Russell nodded but didn't say anything.

"If I had a Shakespeare quote on forgiveness in my head right now, I would use it."

Russell smiled, "When thou dost ask me blessing, I'll kneel down and ask forgiveness," he said quietly.

How is that even English? Trixie thought.

"Yeah, that," she said.

"So have you found your horse?" he asked, and gestured to Casino.

"No."

"What? You had a brilliant lesson."

"Casino isn't my horse. There was no siren song."

"Excuse me?"

"A Siren is a powerful woman with an angelic voice who lives in the sea and sings songs to lure men in."

"What does that have to do with horses?" Russell asked.

"There was no song from Casino. I'm not lured."

"So which horse does sing?"

Trixie opened her mouth to say 'Slow-Moe', but stopped before the words left her vocal cords. There had been no song from him either; he had been a sweet horse to ride, but not her destiny.

Russell, for all his anger and aloofness, still seemed to have that invisible connection to Trixie. He seemed to read her mind. "So, no horse at Apley. Maybe it's time to get your own."

Was it?

After Kaela had handed Quiet Fire over to Moira, she and Amy walked home. As much as she hated to leave early, she had begun to see Amy as a blessing in disguise. Kaela had a lot of homework and she was already falling behind in maths; her father would ban her from the stable if she failed. Not to mention she still had to write an article for the school newspaper. Kaela was sub-editor of the newspaper, and along with editing the articles of all the other journalists, she was expected to hand in one of her own. So far she had nothing but a title. And she wasn't even sure that title was working. Amy forcing her to go home early meant only good things.

Except for the fact that Amy was feeling a little depressed with homesickness for her parents.

"Maybe you should go for a swim," Kaela said in an attempt to cheer her up.

"I don't really like swimming," Amy said.

"Maybe you should play with the dogs."

"They are too big and too rough."

That was true: Lakota and Breeze were Alaskan malamutes so they were already almost Amy's size. Also, their version of fun was to stand on their hind legs and see how quickly they could push humans over. You had to take out life insurance just to play with those mad mutts.

Kaela was about to suggest a new idea when she heard

hooves coming towards them. She looked up to see Mouse and Bart taking a leisurely stroll.

"Hello little one and even littler one," he said with a smile.

"Hi," Amy called, "where did you go?"

"Just went along the roads. Need to strengthen Mouse's legs, he's been slacking lately," he flashed Amy a smile and looked at Kaela, "Why are you going home so early?"

"Homework," Kaela said.

"Well I'll leave you to it then," he said and nudged Mouse back into a walk.

"Bye," Amy called.

Bart turned in the saddle to wave. Out of the corner of her eye Kaela could see that he was looking at her with a sort of sad intensity.

She turned to look at him and smiled. He returned the smile with mild iciness.

"Are you mad because yesterday I walked in on you when you were in the bathroom?" she teased.

"No, I'm a boy, that stuff doesn't bug us. That's why we don't lock the doors."

"Ewww," Kaela said and made a face.

Bart giggled and sauntered off.

Kaela was slowly learning that humour was the best way to communicate with Bart.

"Why is he walking Mouse on the roads?" Amy asked, bringing Kaela out of her daydream.

"If you walk a horse on a hard road, it strengthens the muscles in their legs so by the time you start working them in the ring over jumps and stuff like that, the muscles in their legs are fully developed," Kaela explained.

"Oh."

A minute later Amy had returned to her sombre state.

"Maybe you should watch a movie," Kaela suggested.

"I don't feel like watching a movie."

Finally, out of sheer desperation Kaela went into the garage and dug out her old TV games console with all the coloured cartridges.

"Can that thing even be hooked up to new TVs?" her grandmother asked.

"I hope so."

Kaela's grandmother had moved in almost ten years ago to help raise her after her mother disappeared. She still lived in the Willoughby home although her duties were becoming fewer and fewer every day. This saddened a part of Kaela. Not because she missed her grandmother's constant henpecking or because she was lamenting her lost childhood. It simply meant there were more years between herself and her mother.

Kaela hooked up the old TV games, put in some game she remembered from her childhood and left Amy to her own devices. She retreated to her room, played Jamiroquai as loud as she could stand it, and wrote her article and did her homework. Two hours later Amy was still playing the games with a goofy grin on her face.

"You can't beat the classics," Kaela said with a giggle.

Angela raced across the room to her phone, slipping on the wet floor and sprawling over Copernicus.

"Move, dog. Hello?"

"Hi Ang," Trixie said, "Are you busy?"

"Just got out of the shower. What's up?"

"How did you know when you were ready for your own horse?"

"I didn't, my parents just decided to buy me one. And even then it took months before we found Fergie and even longer before we found Dawn. Why?"

"Do you think you were ready?"

"Of course."

"Do you think I am ready?"

Angela was quiet. She imagined the way Trixie was around the stable. She studied and brought up a verdict.

"Your silence is incriminating."

Angela chuckled, "I think you understand the amount of work involved, therefore you are ready."

"But?"

"But, I think you are living in a bit of a fantasy world concerning the type of dressage horse you want."

"Meaning?"

Angela thought how best to explain, "Ahh, meaning that

you aren't taking into account price range or the fact that the best horse for you could need training."

"I don't want to waste time training though."

"Where are you going in such a hurry?"

Trixie was quiet, but then she finally she admitted, "I don't know."

The girls spoke for a few more minutes and then hung up.

Angela quickly dried herself and especially her hair, which, with all its dripping, had caused a massive wet spot on the bed that Angela would have to attack with a hairdryer. Before she managed to get dressed, her phone rang again.

She tripped over the dog when racing for it.

"*Move,* dog! Hello?"

"Hey Ang, did you see the whole thing with Bart today? Firstly, I'm amazed that saddle supported him, it is a compliment to my tacking abilities. You know, Quiet Fire isn't the easiest tack. He is huge, and I mean huge. Like, that belly is gigantic. If we get stranded on a desert island, I say we eat him: it's the only way to survive. Except that I'm vegan so I can't eat him. What in the name of Pan would I eat on a desert island? What is a desert island? Aren't they all tropical? And if that's the case, I'll have a lot to eat. Secondly, wow! Did you see him on that saddle? It was like something from a fantasy novel. Except of course, I was on a horse instead of a dragon and he was balancing on the stirrup instead of flying with his own wings. Anyway, I feel like the next move is mine. Am I crazy for wanting to go up to him and do the same? Hopefully his tack supports me. It'll be an insult to his tacking abilities if it doesn't. Which is weird because he kind of taught me to tack. How has one advanced and not the other? That is assuming his saddle slips. What if my foot can't reach the stirrup? Mouse is rather tall. Ang? Are you there?"

"Are you high on Jamiroquai?" Angela asked. She could hear the British band playing in the background.

"Maybe a little. Been listening to them since I got home."

"Turn the music off," Angela said calmly.

The blaring sounds stopped and instantly Kaela was calmer. Where everyone else in the world went to dizzying heights from sugar, Kaela just needed Jamiroquai.

Angela understood, she had the same problem with her favourite band. Although, Angela might be slightly worse.

"Okay, now we can talk. What was he whispering to you while defying gravity?"

"Ahhhh, that I looked good while jumping."

"Well then, there is your opening. Do the same to him and tell him he looks good doing whatever."

"He never really rides, or at least he doesn't when I'm around. I did see him walking Mouse on a tar road today though."

"Really? He was speaking to me yesterday about the Season at Equestrian International."

"The *Season* Season? As in, a massive competition every two weeks and if you do well, your future career on horseback is carved in stone?"

70

"The very one."

"What was he talking about?" Kaela asked.

"He was asking me if it was hard and if he should start training now."

"Training? You think he is going to take part?"

"Maybe. He was also asking me about the amount of money they pay you when you win." Angela gave up hope of trying to dry her hair with a towel, and so flopped back onto the bed.

"They pay you?"

"Yes, probably not as much as the entire Season costs you to compete in."

"Where does all your money go? You must be rich by this point."

Angela shrugged, "Into a bank account and forgotten."

"Forgotten?"

"What do I need it for?"

"I would go ballistic ... There are so many books out there that need to be bought and read and studied."

"When you start competing, I hope your father puts your winnings in a bank account you can't touch until you are wiser with money." Angela laughed.

"Me too."

The girls bade each other goodnight and hung up.

Angela attacked the wet spot with her hairdryer.

Her mobile beeped a notification from LetsChat. She quickly checked it out.

Phoenix: ANG! HELP! PLEEEEEEEEEE-AAAAAASE ask your mom if there is a way to get a rocket off a planet without using fossil fuels. Thank you.

Angela hung her head out of her bedroom, "Mom, is there a way to get stuff into space without polluting our planet with dead dinosaurs?"

"Fusion," her mother called back.

Angela: She says 'Fusion'.

Phoenix: Thank you so much. Maybe I'll actually be able to get these characters off their stupid planet now.

Angela: Being a writer sounds hard. I'll stick to horses.

Phoenix: It is hard! I've had to get addicted to some weird fruit I have never seen before, and now I dream about it at night! I'M DREAMING ABOUT FRUIT! This play has made me lose my mind!!!!!!!!

Apparently.

From: trixie-true@feaguemail.co.za
To: kaelalw2000@feaguemail.co.za; phoenix-wfeather@feaguemail.com; horsecrazyang@feaguemail.co.za
Subject: Horse Trial #3

Dear kodas,

What can I say? Casino was perfect. The most brilliant horse for dressage. But apparently there is a difference between the most perfect horse and the most perfect horse for me.

Casino and I just didn't feel it.

My new problem, of course, is that there are no more horses to ride.

TWO SOLUTIONS

1) Go back to Slow-Moe and train him.

2) Get my own horse.

PROS AND CONS OF EACH SOLUTION

1) I don't want to waste time training a horse, I want to advance. I think Slow-Moe belongs in my past. I feel in my bones there is something new waiting for me. I can almost hear that siren's song, you could say.

2) I have discussed my predicament with my parents in the past. They are both of the opinion that horses are expensive and I might as well be asking for the pot at the end of a rainbow. I'm not bothering to ask them now.

CONCLUSION
I don't know.

TOMORROW'S EXPERIMENT
I don't know.

P.S. I'm really confused right now.

⧼ Seven ⧽

There was only one horse left to ride and Trixie bravely asked for him.

"Okay, you can ride Toby today but if one thing doesn't look right to me, then you drop the whole idea," Wendy said reluctantly.

"Thank you; it'll be a great lesson."

"Yeah, let's hope so," Wendy said with a sigh.

Trixie noticed that Wendy's British accent was more pronounced. This was not a good thing. Wendy had moved to South Africa when Bart was still a baby and she had quickly lost her accent, it now only came out when she was either really nervous, or really angry. Trixie wasn't so sure she wanted to know what was making Wendy nervous enough to pull a long forgotten accent from the deep recesses of her brain.

"Well go tack him up, he's not going to do it himself," Wendy said.

Trixie walked to the tack room with heavy feet, the thought of riding Toby scared her. He was a big horse and kept in the advanced classes for a reason.

Come on Beatrix, you have to try him, you can't ride at this level forever, she told herself.

She grabbed Toby's saddle and bridle and made her way to his stall. The horses at Apley Towers were trained to be still and calm while being tacked or groomed, so either exercise could be done in the stall itself without putting the rider in any danger. But Trixie didn't want to risk it: one look at those hooves and she ran to fetch a halter and two lead ropes. She then put Toby on cross ties in the corridor.

"Hey Toby, I need to tack you quickly in case someone needs to get past," Trixie said nervously.

She decided to go the opposite way around and put the saddle on first, that way he was still motionless when she put on the hardest part of the tack. She grabbed his saddle and lifted it, only to discover that Toby was a good two hands taller than Slow-Moe.

She couldn't reach!

"Oh for the love of all things equine," she cried.

There was a footstool for riders to use when mounting exceptionally tall horses, but it was bolted to the ground. For Trixie to use it she would have to take Toby over, and there was no place to put him on cross ties.

"What in Epona's name am I supposed to do now?"

Toby looked at her questioningly.

"Maybe this isn't such a good idea," Trixie said in panic.

"Miss King, would you like some help?" A voice called out to her.

Trixie looked over at the smiling face of Joseph, one of the grooms. If Trixie had not had a saddle in her hands, she would have hugged him right then and there.

"Yes, please. He's too tall," she moaned.

"Why do you have him on cross ties, did you groom him?" Joseph asked, taking the saddle.

"No, I was too scared to tack him up in the stall."

Joseph put the saddle on Toby's back, bent down and pulled the girth over and buckled it in place in a matter of ten seconds.

"Old Toby is a gentleman, he would never put you in any danger," Joseph said, giving Toby's bay neck a pat. His face had the look of admiration it got when he looked at any of the school horses.

While Joseph distracted Toby, Trixie grabbed his bridle and put it on, she then unclipped the lead lines and took the halter off quicker than Joseph had put the saddle on.

Joseph took the halter and lead ropes and went on his merry way.

Trixie nervously watched him go.

"Trot on," Wendy called as all the intermediate riders walked around her.

Kaela automatically picked up the pace. So far, Kaela was having a good lesson; Wendy had put them through some exercises at a walk. Although Quiet Fire had been getting bored with the slow pace (he was bred for speed, of course), he had behaved well and Kaela had spent most of the lesson praising him. She now noticed that he was trotting as though he were on show. She praised him more.

Wendy had them trot around the ring several times before giving them more direction.

"I want you to spread out a bit more, I want two horse lengths between you and the rider in front of you," she called to the five riders in the ring.

Kaela gave the command for Quiet Fire to quicken his pace in order to give space to the riders behind her. Quiet Fire took the pressure from her legs as an invitation to speed up too much. He broke into a canter but Kaela had anticipated the move and brought him back to a trot before his hind legs had caught up with his front ones. Usually that would have looked sloppy, but Kaela and Quiet Fire were riding so well that it could have been a dressage move.

"Well done Kaela, that looked good," Wendy called.

Both Kaela and Quiet Fire beamed.

Bella rode behind Kaela and also moved KaPoe forward, Russell and Jasmyn hung back and spread out from one another. Trixie remained in her place.

"Good work everyone," Wendy called, "you are all riding like pros."

"Probably because we are doing such easy stuff," Bella muttered.

They hung at a trot for a while, Kaela let her concentration lapse and Quiet Fire slowed down.

"Watch it! There are riders behind you," Bella snapped.

Kaela opened her mouth to give Bella a tongue-lashing but Wendy interrupted.

"Shush Bella, you'll affect KaPoe. Kaela, if you're in front you cannot let your horse go on his own mission. You have to be in control all the time. Do you want to swap with Bella?"

"No," Kaela snapped.

She recentred herself and picked up where she'd left off.

"Trixie, you okay?" Wendy asked.

"Yes," Trixie said, but her voice was strained.

As Kaela rounded the corner, she turned her head slightly to the left and looked at Trixie. She was riding well – she was in perfect alignment and her hands were soft, but her face gave her away – it was hard with tension. As Quiet Fire went straight, Kaela brought her face forward.

"Well done Kaela, that was an excellent turn," Wendy called. "Did you see how she turned her head slightly in the direction Quiet Fire was turning? The shift in weight made him curve his body perfectly," Wendy said to the other riders.

Kaela beamed again – sure it was a mistake, but it was a lucky mistake.

When she reached the next turn, she turned her head and Quiet Fire turned out of formation. She pulled him back in line but without the grace of her former movement.

"Now you're thinking about it too much. Relax. Don't think about it, just do it," Wendy said to her.

When she got to the next corner, Kaela turned to look at Trixie.

"There, that's better," Wendy called. "Okay Kaela, you're gonna come down the middle and change diagonals."

Kaela put pressure with her left calf and pulled the left rein towards her abdomen, Quiet Fire turned and trotted down the middle of the ring. Once they got to the fence, Kaela brought her right leg forward, put her left leg behind the girth and turned her horse right. Once he was in a straight line, she double bounced and rode on the right diagonal. The riders were now riding in the opposite direction. Wendy had them change diagonals several times before moving them to a quicker pace.

"Why are we having such an easy lesson?" Bella asked. She glanced quickly at Trixie and Toby. Kaela also had a sneaking suspicion that the lesson was easy because of her friend.

"You are doing easy things so that I can spot your mistakes and fix them," Wendy said.

"But this is all easy stuff we learnt long ago, I haven't made any mistakes," Bella answered.

"Your leg is too stiff – it's amazing KaPoe hasn't broken into a canter with all the banging that's going on. Your heel isn't low enough, you are rising too high out of the saddle, you're moving your hands too much, your alignment is wrong and so far you have not been able to get KaPoe to bend around corners correctly."

Kaela snorted, Bella deserved that.

"Canter on," Wendy called.

Kaela tightened her grip with her legs, placed her rear end deeper into the saddle and gave a little nudge with her left heel. Quiet Fire sometimes started a canter on the wrong leg, so it was the rider's duty to remind him which leg was supposed to lead. Kaela gave a gentle tug on the right rein in order to get Quiet Fire's right leg to lead; she looked down at his shoulders and saw that he had started off on the right leg. For about the millionth time that day, Kaela beamed.

"Prepare to half-halt," Wendy called, Kaela tightened her grip on the reins. "And half-halt."

Kaela gently pulled the reins towards her abdomen, lifted her seat a fraction of an inch out of the saddle and relaxed the grip with her legs. Quiet Fire came back to a trot.

"Prepare to canter … and canter."

Wendy had them canter, trot, walk, trot, walk, trot, canter, trot, canter, trot, walk, trot, canter.

"Okay, last thing for the day … change diagonals."

Kaela turned Quiet Fire to the right and cantered him down the middle of the ring; at the fence she turned him left. He was now cantering on the wrong leg. She needed to perform a flying change in order to get him on the right leg. Kaela leaned back a little and pushed her weight slightly to the right. She gently tugged at the right rein and let the left rein go slightly limp while putting her left leg against the girth and moving her right leg behind the girth. She then squeezed with both legs, and Quiet Fire lifted into the air. Not one of his feet were on the ground. Girl and horse flew. Then he came down again and cantered on the correct leg.

Toby was brilliantly trained, a born show horse. But Trixie could tell that something was not right. The bay gelding had an agitated air to him, almost as though he was electrified. Trixie feared that touching him would electrocute her.

"Prepare to half-halt … and half-halt," Wendy called.

Kaela brought Quiet Fire back to a trot; Bella brought KaPoe back to a trot; as Trixie performed the aids for a half-halt, Toby sped up. She jerked on the right rein to avoid crashing into KaPoe, she tugged on the reins again but Toby ignored her. He sped past Quiet Fire. Kaela reached over and tried to grab his reins, but Toby threw his head in the opposite direction and they were out of her reach. From the look of his shoulders, Trixie could see that he was preparing to gallop. She pulled at the reins once more and when that didn't work, she tugged at the right rein. Toby spun around and prepared to bolt, but Trixie pulled at the reins before he could move; instead he bucked. It was obvious he was bucking to get Trixie off, but Trixie's legs held her in place. She pulled at his reins to get his head up so that he could not counterbalance his hooves. He spun around again and bucked her right off.

"Trixie!" Kaela screamed.

She flew through the air, knowing she was going to land on her back. This was the type of fall they warned you about: the fall that could change your life forever, or end it. In mid-air, Trixie threw her shoulder out so that she spun. She crashed onto the ground on her right side and rolled into a ball to avoid being hit by a hoof as Toby first jumped over her then raced away. She could see Kaela dismounting and Wendy rushing forward. She watched as Toby jumped the fence and galloped off to the feeding paddock.

"Are you okay?" Wendy asked.

Trixie thought about her body for the first time – her legs were fine, she could wiggle her toes (or at least she thought she could), her back was not sore, her coccyx had not suffered any damage and her head was fine. Her shoulder and arm were grazed, but she had suffered worse.

"I'm fine, just shell-shocked."

Kaela knelt down and ripped Trixie's boots and socks off, "Can you move them?" she practically screamed.

Trixie watched in relief as all ten little toes – her piggies, as her mother called them – danced to her brain's command.

"Yes, Kaela, I can move my toes."

"Do you know why he acted like that?" Wendy asked.

Trixie laughed, typical Wendy – always thinking of the horse.

As she pushed herself up, a bolt of pain shot through her right arm. She looked down, expecting her arm to be broken.

"What's wrong?" Kaela asked.

"I think my arm is broken," she held it up, but it looked in perfect form, it didn't even hurt unless she wiggled her hand.

Wendy ran her hand over the arm, "I think you've just sprained your wrist. Come on, we can phone your mother to come get you and take you to the hospital to make sure."

Trixie got up slowly, her muscles were beginning to ache. Wendy grabbed her boots and socks.

Kaela stared at a blonde figure walking towards the feeding paddock.

"What's Angela doing?" Jasmyn asked as she rode past.

"I think she's fetching Toby."

Kaela remounted and followed the riders.

Trixie took the walk of shame to Wendy's office to phone her mother.

❧

"Here Toby," Angela cooed. "Come Toby, come on boy."

He hadn't bothered to jump the fence surrounding the

feeding paddock, and stood grazing on the patch of grass just outside the enclosure. She walked right up to him and got a hold of his bridle. As she began walking back with him, he jerked his head up and out of her reach. She lost control of the reins, and Toby galloped away and jumped the fence into the paddock. Angela climbed over the fence and tried to get his reins again. He trotted away from her.

"You annoying little brat, come here," she cooed.

When she finally got hold of his reins, she climbed on his back so that he couldn't get away from her again.

First he spun to the left, then he spun to the right, then he bucked, but he could not get rid of her. Angela knew that there had to be something wrong with him: she sometimes rode in the advanced class and Toby had never behaved like this.

"What's wrong boy?" she ran her fingers over his coat but couldn't feel anything. She didn't want to risk getting down and inspecting his legs, "But somebody who has a problem with their legs would never be able to buck like that."

To answer her, Toby bucked again. Before he was even out of his buck, Angela kicked him sharply. Toby sprang forward into a hand gallop; she kicked him again for more speed. He flew forward, she kicked him again, he went even faster. She kicked again, this time he did not increase his speed. He couldn't – he was going as fast as he could. Angela held him at that speed until his neck was dripping with sweat, then she let him slow down. On his own, Toby went from gallop to canter. Angela asked him for a flying change, he ignored her. She asked him again. He ignored her and quickened his pace. She asked him once more, when he ignored her she gave him a new command. She did a half-halt, changed diagonals on trot, went back into a canter and then into a serpentine motion. They performed another half-halt and Angela asked for a piaffe, a half-pass, a pirouette and a passage; complicated dressage moves that he performed with flair.

"I'll give you orders until you forget that you don't want to do a flying change," Angela said through clenched teeth.

When she asked for a flying change for the fourth time, he performed it without a hitch.

She jumped the fence and rode him at a walk to the road: he was badly in need of an outride.

"What was wrong with him?" Jasmyn asked. They were already coming back from the outride.

"I think he was just bored with the lesson," Angela answered.

Kaela turned Quiet Fire around and walked back up the road with Angela.

"How did you know he was bored?" she asked.

"When I asked him to do advanced dressage, he behaved well. I think he was just acting up because he was trained to do one thing and somebody was making him do another," Angela said. She gave Toby a pat.

"Kind of like graduating from medical school and then someone puts you in a room and asks you to name shapes for a living?" Kaela asked.

"Exactly like that. He probably thought that was his fate, so he was just revolting."

"I don't think he can be ridden in the advanced class, he's practically asleep," Kaela exclaimed.

Angela leaned down and looked at Toby's face. Sure enough the bay gelding had his eyes closed, "How does he know where he is going?"

"I think he's relying on you."

"That's way too trusting," Angela said as the two entered the riding school again.

"Look at that horse! You're going to have to throw him in the washing machine," Derrick, the head groom, called as the two girls came back.

Kaela looked across at Toby; he was covered in sweat and the dust that he had kicked up from the field.

"It's just sweat, it'll come right off," Angela said as she dismounted.

"Ah Derrick, we have a problem," Kaela said.

"There are no problems, only situations that need solutions," Derrick said.

Angela raised her eyebrows at him and hoped Kaela would let the statement pass, "Okay, we have a situation that needs a solution."

"And what would that be?"

"Toby is exhausted, he can't be ridden any more. So you're one horse short for the advanced class."

"No we're not, one poor rider is going to be late for class because you took an extra-long outride, but we're not short."

"What do you mean?"

"Moira's on holiday, so Quiet Fire would have had the afternoon off but now he's got to take Toby's place."

Angela looked over at Kaela and Quiet Fire; Angela assumed that she had completely forgotten that he had to be ridden in class. Kaela handed the reins to Derrick and followed Angela to Toby's stall. The horse was so tired that they didn't even need to tie him up; he just stood there and had a bath.

"So now what does Trixie do?" Angela asked.

"There are no other open dressage horses, she's either got to learn to control Toby or she will have to stick to Slow-Moe," Kaela said.

"Or she could just get her own horse," Angela suggested.

"How many times have I sat here with you?"

"Too many."

Trixie looked around the oh-so-familiar waiting room of the emergency care. Granted, this was the first time they had been there this year, but Trixie was surely no stranger.

"When were we here last?" her mother asked.

"When Slow-Moe refused the jump at the Christmas

competition and I flew face first into the jump. Broken nose. Blood everywhere."

"Oh yes, Christmas Eve in the emergency room is always high on my priorities list."

"Better than the one before that, remember? When I fell and got my foot caught in the stirrup?"

"Oh yes, when you got dragged across the riding ring."

"I'm the only one at Apley who can boast about that."

"Why don't you girls do nice sweet things like baking or ballet? Why do you all climb on top of giant animals that want to hurt you?"

"They do not want to hurt us. And can you honestly see me doing ballet or baking?"

Her mother sighed, "You would burn the kitchen down, and, at ballet, you would probably pull on the rope that says, 'do not pull', and bring the roof down on everybody."

"It'd save the audience from having to watch the production."

"Beatrix King," a doctor called from the doorway.

Trixie and her mother hopped up and followed him to his office.

"I am Dr Mohammed, what can I do for you today?"

Trixie was about to tell the story when her eyes fell on a family picture on the doctor's desk, "Shanaeda!" she cried.

The doctor looked at her with big eyes and then down at the picture of his daughter.

"She rides at my stable," Trixie explained excitedly.

Dr Mohammed laughed, "Oh okay. I thought you were stalking me there for a second. So I assume it was a horse riding injury that brought you here?"

"Yes, I fell and landed funny. And now my wrist is really sore."

"Are you in shock?"

Trixie shrugged, "I suppose I am a little disappointed that I fell, I was hoping to conquer the mighty horse. But no, I wouldn't say I am shocked, I fall all the time."

Dr Mohammed smiled, "Well that answers that question. Want to hop on the bed, just so I can check that you are fine and there is nothing internal?"

"I am hoping I have something internal. Stomach, spleen, intestines, liver, they sound important, Doc."

"I think I know which rider you are. Shanaeda always talks about the blonde with the cheeky answers for everything."

"That'll be Trixie," her mother said.

Trixie lay down on the bed while Dr Mohammed took her temperature, blood pressure, checked her eyes and listened to her lungs. Finally he pressed his fingers into her abdomen to make sure there was no internal pain or bleeding.

"You're as fit as a horse," he proclaimed when he was done. "Now, let's look at this wrist."

"About time, that's the reason I came in here," Trixie said with a smile.

Dr Mohammed laughed at her while her mother shook her head and rolled her eyes.

"So which horse did you fall from?"

"Toby."

He looked at her in surprise, "The big dark brown one with the star?"

"You know him?"

"Shanaeda wants him."

Trixie grabbed his wrists, "No, Doc. For all that is sweet and chocolatey in this world, do not let Shanaeda near him. She would fit nicely under one hoof."

"I am sure he is just misunderstood, all he needs is a hug."

Trixie stared at the doctor with big eyes.

"You see, you are not the only one who can make jokes," the doctor added.

Trixie laughed and hopped off the bed as Dr Mohammed returned to his desk.

"Her wrist is just sprained. It will be sore for a few days, but there is nothing we can do about it. Frankly I would be more worried about those grazes all over the right-hand side of her body." He turned to look at Trixie, "When you have a bath tonight, put some salt in the water. It will disinfect the scrapes and heal the wounds quicker. Other than that, just take it easy for the rest of the night. Shock may still come later and if that happens, just lie down in a quiet room with low lighting and have some tea."

Trixie's mother nodded, "Anything else?"

"Don't ride misunderstood horses."

"Unfortunately that is the only choice at the moment.

Until I find the right one for me, I have to ride the rest of them."

"You have the right one," her mother said.

"I've outgrown him, I need a new one."

"Oh I am so not looking forward to this conversation when Shanaeda wants a horse," Dr Mohammed said with a slow shake of his head.

"I'm not shopping for a horse, just looking for one in the confines of Apley," Trixie said, raising her eyebrows at her mother.

"Maybe you should widen your search: might be safer than riding Apley's misunderstood horses that have no current riders."

"I agree doctor."

Dr Mohammed frowned at her, "Didn't I treat you for a broken nose a few months ago?"

Kaela sat on the railing, pulling off the leaves from the nearby tree while she spoke to Trixie over the phone.

"So it was just sprained?"

Kaela had had a mad moment where the reality of horse riding had come crashing down on her. Trixie could have gotten seriously hurt. She could have dislocated her shoulder or even broken it. Or broken her neck. Or a million other horrid things that could happen when you're riding.

Kaela's mother had gone out riding one day and had never come home. The horse was found wandering the family farm graveyard.

Anything could happen.

"Yup, not even a bad sprain, the doctor said he is more concerned with the grazes on my shoulder. Of course, my mother had a cadenza over those. She poured an entire packet of salt in my bathtub. And then I made the mistake of opening my eyes under water," Trixie explained. "And I'm now officially forbidden from riding Toby."

"That's stupid, something like that could have happened with any horse."

"Yes, well by the way my mother was acting, I'm lucky that I'm still allowed to ride. I could see she wanted to hit the doctor when we were talking about Toby."

"So now what are you going to do about riding?"

"I'm gonna have to stick with Slow-Moe, there are no other horses to ride. Maybe I could train him," Trixie said with fake excitement.

"What about the idea for your own horse?"

"Who are we kidding, Kaela? My parents would never get me my own horse. At the rate I'm going, I'm not entirely sure I want my own horse."

"Why?"

Trixie was quiet for a second, "What if I find a horse that I like, buy it and then it ends up being like Toby? He doesn't want to do easy dressage so he bucks me off."

94

"So find a horse that still needs training."

"But I don't want to waste time training."

"Something has to give, Trix. You have to make some sacrifices to move forward."

"I don't want a horse that doesn't give me the siren's song."

"Then stick with Slow-Moe till you hear that song."

"So he just started bucking?" Trixie's father asked.

"Yes, he was bored so he wanted me off his back," Trixie explained.

"I'd also want you off my back. You're lucky he didn't see your face, imagine what he would have done to you then," Melody, Trixie's elder sister, said.

"He probably bucked because he was downwind of you," Trixie replied scathingly.

"At least I don't smell like a horse," Melody said in a sing-song voice while she dished herself some salad.

"Hey, no fighting at the table," Trixie's mom said. "Melody, would you please pass the pepper?"

"So are you going to ride this horse tomorrow?" Her father asked.

"Certainly not. She is never riding that horse again."

"Mom, it could have happened with any horse. It wasn't Toby's fault. I really should have known better than to ride him in the first place."

"So then *why* were you riding him?" her father asked.

"I rode him because there are no other horses at Apley Towers that I can ride. He was my last hope."

"That stable is full of horses. I'm sure there is one for you to ride," her father said.

"No there isn't. You either get dressage horses or jumping horses. I can only choose from the dressage horses, and only from the ones without intermediate riders." Trixie flicked the lettuce on her plate with her fork, barely looking at her parents.

"I don't understand why you don't just stick to Slow-Moe," her mother sighed.

Trixie shrugged, "I suppose I have to," she said sadly, "there are no other horses. There is nothing I can do."

Her mother and father looked at each other with raised eyebrows.

"How did Kaela react when you fell?" her mother finally asked.

Trixie shrugged, she hadn't been paying attention.

"Someone close to her falling from their horse must always jolt her," her mother said, "she probably sat there being reminded of her mother's fall."

"Maybe," Trixie said, she didn't feel like thinking about it or anything. Kaela was getting sympathy whilst she was getting a lecture. Who had fallen off the horse? Trixie or Kaela?

She felt emotionally exhausted.

And she wasn't feeling well either. Bile climbed her throat. She raced from the table and into the bathroom. She made it to the toilet just in time to vomit.

The shock had eventually found her.

Kaela sat in her father's study going through Bart's LetsChat account. Unlike all her female friends, Bart was not particularly talkative. He put up very few statuses and hardly ever put up photos.

But she liked to see his profile picture. It was of Mouse who, for some unknown reason, had his tongue stuck out and his eyes closed. It made her laugh because Bart's personality shone through in every pixel. Only his giddy nature could bring out a funny face in a horse.

Her father's computer started beeping as she began wondering how to match the stirrup act he had pulled. Kaela answered the video call from Phoenix.

"Well hello stranger."

"Have you seen the movie *The Secret Garden?*" Phoenix asked.

"Yes. The book was better."

"Well you sound just like that little girl."

"She's British. I am South African."

"If I had a British accent, I would never stop talking."

"I don't have a British accent. But trust me, I never stop

talking," said Kaela. Even though she had now decided that she was actually rather quiet in comparison with Amy.

"Okay, I need to tell you something, and then you can just pass the news on to the other kodas. But promise you won't laugh?"

"I won't laugh. Maybe."

"A few weeks ago, I enrolled in a riding school."

"Why? You already know how to ride."

"I know how to ride like a Native. I wanted to learn how to ride with a saddle. But no bit, just a hackamore. Anyway, no one on the rez could teach me so I joined a riding school in town."

"That's great. Are you having fun? Are you using Wind Whistler?"

"No. She hasn't been trained with a saddle. I'll ride the school horses until I decide where I want to go. But, I've just been told that the riding school is competing, and I'm competing with them. Not only have I only recently learnt how to do courses, but now I'm about to be judged on them."

"Practise, practise, practise and you will be fine!" Kaela said excitedly.

Honestly, Kaela didn't understand what Phoenix was worried about. She was nearly as good as Angela on horseback. It wouldn't surprise her in the least if Phoenix walked away with the blue ribbon.

"I'm scared to death. What if I mess up and everyone laughs at me?"

"What if you don't mess up and you win?"

"I don't think I can do it. I think I'm too scared."

Kaela smiled at her friend, "Can I tell you what my father tells me every time I don't want to do something because I'm scared?"

"Yes."

"Do it now, or forever wish you had!"

"Here is your tea. Sip it slowly, we don't want it coming back up again."

Trixie watched through swollen lids as her mother put the cup of tea on her nightstand, then sat down on her bed. Her weight pulled the covers so tight that Trixie began to feel claustrophobic.

"No school or riding tomorrow," she said.

Trixie nodded, but she wondered why her mother wouldn't just leave her alone. Why did she hang about when all Trixie wanted to do was sleep?

"Is the room cool enough?"

Trixie nodded.

"Are you comfortable?"

Trixie nodded.

"Do you need anything?"

Trixie shook her head.

"Why are you so desperate to find a new horse? Are you feeling like you have to compete with Angela?"

"No," she croaked, "I just wanted to do more dressage. Slow-Moe couldn't do it. But it's fine. I'll stick with Slow-Moe, at least then I don't fall."

"You have fallen off Slow-Moe at least twice a month for the last few years."

"But I'm used to Slow-Moe, I'm not used to other horses."

"Can Wendy sell Slow-Moe? Or will he always be at the stable?"

"Anything can happen. He could be sold, he could get sick."

"And then what happens?"

Trixie shrugged, "Have to find a new horse."

"So we'll be back in the emergency room?"

Trixie shrugged, she was struggling to stay awake.

"So in other words, your ability to stay safe on a horse rests in the hands of someone else?"

Trixie nodded, although she had no idea what her mother was talking about.

"Well, that's something to think about isn't it?"

Trixie was asleep before her mother had left the room.

❧ Eight ❧

Kaela was late for a meeting with her editor. Nothing new. It happened nearly every meeting. But this time she had outdone herself. She was in fact so late that technically she was running on time for the meeting she had booked after this one.

"Please tell me that the article you are writing has nothing to do with horses or stables?" Tess said as Kaela ran into the office.

"Have I been typecast already?"

"Indeed. You are the Anthony Henry of the high school newspaper world. Even if you don't write about horses, people will assume it is a horse article. Same as Henry and his historical dramas, even though half the time he doesn't even write drama."

Kaela thought about the success of the author in question – book deals, bestsellers lists, movies and entire generations knowing your name – she, as a hopeful writer, could only dream and hope.

"You will be glad to know that my next article is in fact on dragon lore."

"Dragons?"

"Yes," Kaela said with pride.

"The things you can put a saddle on and ride?"

Kaela hadn't thought of that, "Yes," she said slowly, "those things."

"Maybe you deserve your typecast," Tess laughed.

Trixie could not figure what had gone wrong with TV. Who were these fools parading themselves for the masses? Did the public really have to know what embarrassing thing they refused to see a doctor about? Or watch their stomach-turning auditions for singing careers that would take them nowhere? She now knew why she never bothered watching. Even the science shows were littered with inaccuracies. And there was a mathematician who claimed that seven went into twenty-eight only three times.

She sighed in boredom and put her head back, she would have been at school right now. Instead, she was at home with her mother watching bad TV.

She should have just stuck to Slow-Moe.

Her mother had been on the phone for ages: how that

woman did not run out of things to talk about was beyond Trixie. Not even the kodas could talk that much.

Every hour, Kaela would send a text message informing Trixie of every boring thing she was missing. Trixie would reply with the latest piece of junk on TV. After nearly six hours, Kaela had been forced to admit that Trixie had it worse.

At lunchtime, Angela had texted with some fairly interesting news.

Wendy just walked past Dawn's stall and she was on the phone with your mom.

This was news to her. Sabrina King had taken the day off work to care for her sickly daughter, only to spend the day on the phone with said daughter's riding instructor?

Weird.

Boredom eventually overtook Trixie and she fell asleep on the couch, only waking when long shadows clawed across the carpet and her whole family was home.

She dragged her heavy limbs to the kitchen to help her mother and sister cook. Through the window she glanced at her father mowing the lawn and trying to avoid the acorns thrown by the monkeys (obviously they were slightly perturbed by the noise).

"Feeling better?" Her mother asked.

Trixie nodded, although she had a pounding headache.

It was a light supper thankfully, Trixie wasn't sure she could keep something heavy down.

"Do you know that potatoes were once the main ingredient in every meal in the Lake District?" her mother asked as she peeled.

The girls nodded. They had heard this story a million times.

"Even the main ingredient in onion soup. How odd is that? Shouldn't onion be the main ingredient in onion soup?"

Trixie grimaced, the idea of onion soup made her stomach do flip-flops.

"How do you know all this, Mom? You have never even been to England," Melody said.

"My great-grandparents lived in the Lake District before they moved to South Africa."

"And did they eat potatoes every day?"

"Yes, my great-grandfather did. He even took potatoes to work with him: one for him and one for his horse."

Trixie sighed, she would have been cycling home right now instead of talking about potatoes.

Why hadn't she just stuck to Slow-Moe?

When dinner had been made, served and eaten, Trixie asked to be excused.

"No," her mother said, "we need to talk to you."

Oh great, they are going to tell me that I can't ride any more, Trixie thought, *I'm gonna start flinging potatoes.*

"I've been making a few phone calls today. Getting some info, and chatting with your father. And we have decided that we are going to get you your own horse."

Trixie's jaw dropped.

"Oi, what do I get?" Melody cried.

"What do you want?"

"A trip to the cathedrals of Europe?"

Their father snorted.

"How about I convert that old playhouse of yours into an art studio?"

"Deal!" Melody's eyes widened.

"Wait, how can you just decide to get me a horse?" Trixie asked.

Sabrina shrugged, "We have always known that this was something we would have to eventually do."

"We are just happy we only have to buy one horse," her father piped in.

"Thank you, Melody. Thank you for quitting that silly sport so we don't have to buy two horses," Melody teased.

"No, instead I have to build you an art studio."

"But," Trixie interrupted, "am I just going out and buying a horse?"

"Well obviously you have a price cap. And I do not want you buying the first horse you come across. I've already spoken to Wendy, she has been looking for a stallion. She has kindly agreed to take you along with her to find this horse. She will then check it out and make sure it is right for you. But," Sabrina put her finger up as she used to when Trixie was a toddler and misbehaving, "if this takes ages then it takes ages. You will not buy the wrong horse just because you want one by the weekend."

"And, you are sticking to Slow-Moe until you find this dream horse."

Trixie looked from her mother to her father and back again. She didn't know what to say.

"Oh woman, hurry up and burst into tears, scream and say thank you. I want to discuss my art studio."

From: trixie-true@feaguemail.co.za
To: kaelalw2000@feaguemail.co.za; phoenix-wfeather@feaguemail.com; horsecrazyang@feaguemail.co.za
Subject: Horse Win for Team Trixie

Well, howdy do kodas,

EXCITING NEWS
My parents have informed me that I am getting a horse.

YOUR REACTIONS

Angela: Apparently she knew, Wendy told her when she got off the phone with my mom.

Kaela: "I would be more excited for you if I weren't exponentially exhausted from Amy's incessant and indefatigable chatter" (She said that, not me. I didn't even understand half of those words.)

Phoenix: "I swear I dreamt that last night. I bet you it's going be a boy horse with a girl's name. Let me know. If I'm right, I can go into business as a psychic!" (I'm willing to bet that play has officially sent Phoenix bonkers.)

THE PLANS

Tomorrow we are headed out to a few horse farms with Wendy. Angela is busy at show jumping competitions the rest of us will never be good enough for, but Kaela has been formally invited to attend (and she'd better!!).

IN CONCLUSION

It has been an extremely successful experiment.

P.S. Woohoo!

‰ Nine ‰

"Wow, look at the barn," Trixie exclaimed, "so Hollywood."

Kaela looked over at the building; sure enough it was an old school, classic red and white barn – just like in the movies.

"What do you think they keep in there?" Kaela asked.

"Barn stuff," Wendy answered. She was already walking towards the buildings.

"What's 'barn stuff'?" Trixie whispered.

"Don't know," Kaela whispered back.

They had to run to catch up with Wendy.

It was Saturday morning and the girls had gone with Wendy to a livery yard in the Midlands. According to an internet advertisement, they were selling two yearlings and had a few other horses up for sale.

Kaela had been quick to point out that all the land at this livery yard had once belonged to Angela's ancestors in order to protect it from developers.

"Good on them," Wendy had said.

Kaela looked around at the land as it stretched into the craggy hills, eventually becoming the Drakensburg Mountains. She wished Angela was with them to see this.

"Hi," an old man in jeans and a cowboy shirt and hat called, "you must be Ms Oberon."

"Yes, hi," Wendy said, and extended her hand.

The cowboy shook it and greeted her with a big smile; Kaela could see a gold tooth in the bottom row.

"And this is Trixie and Kaela," Wendy said pointing to the girls, "Trixie is looking for a horse."

"Great!" the cowboy exclaimed. "What type of horse are you looking to buy?"

"Preferably one that has had a fair amount of dressage training," Trixie said with sparkling eyes.

"Oh … okay," the cowboy looked very surprised, "well … ah … I was actually asking what type of horse you were after; a mare, a gelding, a grey, a bay – that type of thing."

Kaela's eyebrows shot up. What did the horse's colour matter?

"Oh, I really don't mind," Trixie said with a suspicious glance towards Wendy.

"Why don't you take Trixie to look at the horses and I'll go see the yearlings," Wendy said to the cowboy.

"Yes, they are in the field," he said, pointing just over Wendy's shoulder. "Come on Trixie and Katie, I'll take you to the horses."

"It's Kaela."

"Of course it is."

The girls frowned at each other but they followed him anyway. He led them to the stables where the grooms were mucking out stalls. A beautiful strawberry roan stuck its head over the stall door and Trixie raised her hand to let the horse sniff.

"This is Sea Coral," the cowboy said, "she is up for sale at a very reasonable price."

"Could you please tell me a bit about her?" Trixie asked sweetly.

"Ah, okay … sure … she is, let me think now," the cowboy took his hat off and scratched his bald head. "She is about ten years old, she was owned by a little girl who used to compete with her."

"In dressage?" Trixie asked hopefully.

"Ah … sure, sure, in dressage."

Kaela didn't trust this man one bit, he was either making everything up or he clearly didn't know what he was talking about.

"Is there anything else we should be aware of, like temperaments or allergies? Was she trained with traditional methods or were ulterior ways used?" Kaela said.

"Does she have any fears? How is she with other horses?" Trixie interjected.

The cowboy's grin faulted for a second but then he composed himself and smiled so that the gold tooth showed.

"She is a nice calm horse, she isn't allergic to anything and she was trained traditionally. She doesn't have any fears and she is a darling with other horses. And she is in perfect health."

Sounds like a dream horse, Kaela thought. She had never heard of a horse that did not have fears. That was like finding a human with no fears: impossible.

"Would you mind if I rode her?" Trixie asked sweetly.

The cowboy's smile faltered again, "Of course you can ride her, but she had a busy day yesterday so it's best you stick to a walk."

Trixie's eyes narrowed, "Sure", she said with suspicion.

When the cowboy brought the tack, Trixie held her arms out for it.

"Don't worry your pretty little head, I'll tack her," he said with a toothy grin.

"I'd like to tack her, thanks all the same," Trixie said stubbornly.

The cowboy reluctantly handed the tack over.

The girls let themselves into the stall. Kaela's eyes automatically swept over Sea Coral's body. It didn't look as though there was anything wrong with her, but she didn't trust what she saw. She slowly ran her hands over Sea Coral's legs. There was nothing wrong with them.

There was no grooming kit so Trixie ran her nails through Sea Coral's coat to remove the dust. As far as she could tell, there was nothing wrong with Sea Coral's back.

Kaela took the bridle and put it on the mare's head. As the bit went in, Kaela got a good look at the horse's teeth.

Her teeth were quite triangular and Kaela could almost see a dental star in the centre of each tooth, this meant that the mare was about twelve or thirteen. Older than the Cowboy had said. Kaela pulled Sea Coral's forelock over her headpiece and gave her a hard pat on her red neck. So far Kaela was impressed with her; she was a good horse who looked like she was in a good condition.

She wasn't, however, very impressed with the cowboy. What other information had he gotten wrong?

Trixie lifted the saddle and put in on the mare's back. As she leaned down to get the girth she said, "Sea Coral's stomach is slightly bloated." Trixie ran her hand across the belly, "It doesn't feel swollen". She put her ear against Sea Coral's stomach, "Normal sounds. No colic."

Trixie shrugged and buckled the girth in place.

The girls, the cowboy and Sea Coral made their way to the training ring. Wendy saw them and came over.

"So what's the verdict?" Wendy asked, gesturing towards Sea Coral.

"She's great, very calm. She's about thirteen. But the cowboy over there is not to be trusted," Kaela informed.

"I know what you mean: he said his yearlings were Hanoverians, they looked more like Basuto ponies to me," Wendy said with disappointment.

Trixie walked Sea Coral around the ring; Wendy's eyes hungrily went over the horse. Trixie brought Sea Coral back to Wendy and Kaela.

"He says that I can't go faster than a walk, but how am I supposed to know if I want her if I can't do anything with her?" Trixie asked.

It was clear that Trixie was already in love.

Wendy looked over at the cowboy, "Trixie is going to take her through the paces. Sea Coral looks as though she needs a good work out."

"I don't think that's a good idea," the cowboy said.

"Why not?"

"Because, because … ah … because she worked really hard yesterday and she needs the rest."

On the contrary, Sea Coral looked as though she was relishing her trip outside and couldn't wait to run the back of the wind. Her ears perked forward, her eyes shone in the sunlight; she pawed at the ground with both front hooves as though irritated with the command to stand still.

"Nonsense, she'll be fine," Wendy said, "Trixie, walk, trot, canter, do a few other things if you want but don't jump her."

Trixie nodded happily and trotted off.

"Why mustn't she jump?" Kaela asked.

"I don't think it's a good idea in her condition."

Kaela was about to ask what condition that was but her eyes were automatically drawn to Trixie and Sea Coral. The two looked really good together – Sea Coral had gentle gaits and good form. Trixie put her through the paces and then started on dressage. She asked for a half-halt, Sea Coral came to a complete halt. She asked the mare to extend her trot, the mare ignored her. When Trixie asked for a flying change, Sea Coral did two and ended up on the wrong leg again. Trixie asked for another flying change, Sea Coral tried again but ended up getting her feet caught up in each other and nearly fell. Trixie slowed her down and let her walk on a loose rein for a while.

"Not the right horse," Trixie said sadly.

"You can't pick the first horse you see," Wendy said.

"We still have a few more horses," the cowboy said as Trixie dismounted and handed the reins over to him.

"I don't think we should risk it," Kaela whispered.

"No thanks. I think we'll be on our way now," Wendy said to him.

"Okay, well thanks for coming," the cowboy said with his toothy grin.

Trixie gave Sea Coral a pat, "Take good care of her," she said to the cowboy.

"Will do, will do."

The three waved goodbye as they climbed into the car.

"At least the horses are well cared for," Trixie said.

"Yes, but they are just here for a profit," Wendy said.

Then Kaela remembered what Wendy had said.

"What condition was Sea Coral in?"

Wendy looked over and smiled at her, "She's pregnant."

The next place they visited was a private owner who was selling her horse as she was emigrating. When they arrived, they'd had to check the address to make sure they were at the right place – it definitely didn't look like a horsey place.

There was a huge vegetable garden with a washing line that spread across it. On the washing line were dripping tie-dye shirts, blankets and skirts. As the three got out of the car and looked around, an old woman with bright orange and pink clothes came running out of the house.

"Hi, you made it. So good to see you. Come through, come through. Aquarius is already tacked up."

She led the three through the garden to the back where a small riding ring and a stall sat in the shade of three oak trees.

"Much better," Kaela said.

"Come, come. He's all ready to go."

Trixie followed the woman to the stall. She came out leading a light bay with big droopy eyes.

"Do you think he just woke up?" Kaela asked Wendy.

"Let's hope so."

It was still early in the morning, so it was possible.

Trixie mounted and started warming the horse up. The old lady came over to Wendy and Kaela.

"Hi, I'm Evelyn."

"Wendy. This is Kaela."

"Where are you moving to?" Kaela asked.

"England. I left in the seventies and now I see that the sixties are coming back I have no choice, I have to return."

Kaela had no idea how it was possible for the sixties to come back so she kept her mouth shut and stared at Trixie.

"So what is Aquarius like?" Wendy asked.

"Groovy. He's a hippie horse," Evelyn said excitedly.

Trixie was realising just how much of a hippie horse he was. His mane was untidily plaited with what looked like a peace symbol attached to it. He wasn't very responsive: she would have to ask him several times for a new gait. He wasn't lazy, just incredibly chilled. She leaned down and tickled his ears, he sighed with pleasure.

"Groovy baby," Trixie whispered. He was a lovely horse, and clearly well looked after.

She looked up at Kaela and shook her head.

"Another one bites the dust," Kaela said with a sigh.

The next place they visited wasn't any better. At first Trixie's eyes had widened in amazement when she saw the beautiful Thoroughbred up for sale. But as soon as Trixie was in the saddle, she came to the realisation that this horse was fresh off the track. He was very excited and had no patience for the slow gaits that Trixie wanted. When she asked for a canter, he had bolted. They were in too small an enclosure to gallop and the gelding had to turn very quickly to avoid running into the fence. To stay on, Trixie had to grab onto his mane. The Thoroughbred threw his head up in surprise.

Trixie knew she hadn't hurt him, she had just given him a fright – this horse had probably never had someone pull on his mane before. Definitely not the horse for her.

Next they went to a stud farm. On the internet they had advertised that they were selling three-year-old stallions and mares and an ex-stud, which had been gelded and needed to be rehomed. They arrived to find quite a few people already shopping for horses.

"That's a good sign," Wendy said.

Although the stud farm was clearly a respectable place, Wendy could not find what she was looking for. On the contrary, Kaela had seen at least three stallions she would have bought.

"What about that one?" Kaela said pointing to a beautiful Kladruber with a long straight back.

"He's beautiful, but he looks slightly feral," Wendy said with wide eyes.

Kaela turned to look at the stallion; he had just risen up on his hind legs and was displaying his front legs in a manly fashion. It looked good, but it could be dangerous.

"He's a stallion, they all do that," Kaela said in defence of the beautiful horse.

"It's okay in the field, but if he does that when somebody is trying to handle him …" Wendy didn't finish that sentence, she didn't have to.

"But, in all fairness, all stallions can be wild and dangerous," Kaela said.

"Actually that's not entirely correct," a voice said.

The two turned to look at a dark-haired man walking up to them.

"Hi, I'm Michael," he said holding his hand out.

"Hi, I'm Wendy and this is Kaela," they both shook hands with him.

"What were you saying about stallions?" Kaela asked.

"Contrary to popular belief: they are not vicious, wild animals that should be avoided like the plague. If a stallion is treated right and handled properly from birth, he will be just as easy to handle as a mare or gelding," Michael said.

Kaela smiled, her mother had said the exact same thing. Her stallion, Black Satin, had even competed in the Empire Games with her.

"So how are the stallions treated from birth?" Wendy asked.

Kaela could not help but notice how Wendy flicked her long, blonde hair off her shoulders and put her fingers against her neck.

"We treat our stallions the same way that anybody would treat a mare or gelding. We expect them to behave and treat them accordingly, and that's what we get," he said, pointing to a groom who led a fifteen hand stallion around a group of little girls. The girls were shorter than the stallion's legs and the horse sniffed at them curiously.

"How are the stallions raised?" Wendy asked, tilting her head sideways and smiling.

Kaela frowned at her.

"We use alternative methods of training our horses, as well as alternative healings for when they are sick," Michael said proudly. "We even have our own equine homeopath."

Kaela's ears perked up at that. Her father was a homeopath. Granted, he treated humans not horses, but it was all the same. Homeopathy was magic. Kaela was yet to see it fail.

"What alternative methods?" Kaela asked. The old ways of training horses were sometimes cruel and Kaela, activist that she was, was always open to new ways of doing things.

"We reward the behaviour we do want and ignore the behaviour we don't want. That way a horse looks forward to doing things the way we want because then he, or she, will get praised for it."

"And alternative methods for healing them?" Wendy asked with an extra bat of her eyes.

"Herbs rather than chemicals. There is a natural way to heal every ailment," Michael said.

Wendy looked over at Kaela with surprise. Kaela had been saying those exact same words for years.

"You have a great place, I'll be sure to mention you in the right circles," Kaela said. She couldn't wait to scream about the stud farm from the mountain tops.

"So how many stallions are up for sale?" Wendy asked.

Hair flick, eye bat, tilted head smile.

"Well, I'll show you," Michael said with a smile.

The two walked off, leaving Kaela to stare after them.

"How rude," she exclaimed and went to find her friend.

Trixie had just dismounted a stocky chestnut when Kaela came up to her.

"So how'd it go?" Kaela asked.

"He is a great horse, he is just so calm," Trixie said.

"But?"

"He will make a great dressage horse one day, but today he wouldn't know a dressage signal if it hit him on the head," Trixie said sadly.

"Well, if he would make a good dressage horse, wouldn't you want to train him?" Kaela asked.

"One day I want a horse that I can train my way, but right now I want a horse that already has the basics down and I can take it from there," Trixie said.

"The basics being?" Kaela asked.

"I want a horse that is at Quiet Fire's level and I want to take him to Fergie's level."

Kaela thought about Quiet Fire. True, the horse was well trained in dressage but that had been because of his riders.

"Ah Trixie, I don't think you're going to find a horse that is already trained at that level," Kaela said cautiously.

"Of course I will. I just have to look."

"Think about it," Kaela said as the two walked back to Wendy, "all the dressage horses at Apley Towers have been trained by their riders. Even Fergie came to Angela right off the track."

"So what are you trying to say?" Trixie stopped walking and looked at her.

Kaela stopped walking but knew that staring Trixie in the eye while she was in this mood was dangerous, instead she walked over to the fence and stood up on the first bar, watching the horses in the fields. "When Quiet Fire first came to the stables he was even more of a novice than Eagle is. It was his riders who trained him in their own time and in their lessons."

"So?"

"So, I think you have to seriously consider that when choosing a horse."

"Consider what? That Quiet Fire was trained at Apley? What's that got to do with my horse?"

"I'm just saying, maybe you are asking for the impossible. Or at the very least, the difficult to come by. Quiet Fire and Fergie were trained to be where they are. Maybe, in your price range, you can't get a horse already trained at their level."

"I can't spend extra time training a horse. I need to be getting better at dressage, not spending years getting my horse up to where I am right now. I'm already falling behind."

"I understand that," Kaela argued.

"Do you?" Trixie interrupted, "It's not you that has to make this decision."

Kaela stepped back under the weight of this truth.

"Let's just find Wendy," she said and walked off.

Trixie quickly caught up with her but didn't say anything.

"Write a list then," Kaela eventually said.

"A list?"

"Yes, write a list of exactly what you want in a horse. Maybe that will make this decision easier or something. Or at least make you aware of what you actually do want in a horse."

"Okay, thank you."

Wendy and Michael interrupted with talk of stallions. The girls followed the two to the car in silence.

"Well I'll definitely call you and let you know," Wendy said to Michael as she got into the driver's seat.

"She'll definitely call you," Kaela mumbled.

As the car drove away, Kaela caught a glimpse of the Kladruber, he was once again on his back hooves and throwing his front legs out in front of him. Kaela was enthralled by the beautiful horse; he had a spirit that she had never seen before in any horse. He brought out a smile and a secret hope she didn't know she had. Her quarrel with Trixie was completely forgotten in the face of this majestic animal.

"So, see any stallions you'd like to take home?" Kaela asked with a smile, *a stallion named Michael maybe?*

"No, not really. None really stood out."

"I'm sure at least one stood out," *The one on two legs.*

"No, not really," Wendy said, shaking her head.

Yeah right, Kaela thought and giggled.

"Okay, last place for today," Wendy said as they drove into a riding school near Equestrian International.

"How much must it suck to compete with them?" Kaela asked.

"We all compete with them," Wendy said.

The owner led the three over to a bay mare. Trixie checked if she was pregnant before mounting her.

Once in the ring, Trixie found out why the horse was up for sale – she was extremely stubborn. She refused Trixie's every direction, tossing her head in fury and whipping Trixie on the arms with her long tail. Eventually the mare bolted, but Trixie was too quick for her. Before she got a good rhythm going, Trixie pulled on the right rein and the mare swung around and came to a halt.

"No," Trixie said and dismounted.

"Thanks anyway," Kaela called.

Trixie sighed as the three drove away.

"You've only been looking for one day," Kaela said.

"You'll find one, Trixie," Wendy said.

But thanks to her conversation with Kaela, and her parents' price cap, Trixie had a sneaking suspicion that her standards were a bit too high.

⤚ Ten ⤙

"Hey Trixie-True."

"Hi Dad," Trixie said as she walked into his study.

"How'd horse shopping go?" he asked.

"Well, I could have a pregnant mare that trips on her own feet, a hippie that wishes he lived in London in the sixties, an impatient Thoroughbred who likes to gallop in small spaces, a great chestnut who doesn't know what dressage is or a stubborn mare who bolts and whips," Trixie said with a sigh.

"That bad huh?"

"Yup."

"Well keep looking, you'll find one," her father said.

Maybe.

"Kaela, get dressed we're going out for supper!" Kaela's father called from across the garden.

He, Amy and another woman whom Kaela had never seen before all stood beside the pool playing with Breeze and Lakota. Kaela walked over to them.

"Kaela, this is Niamh," her father said, gesturing towards the woman.

Kaela looked over at the woman: she was tall and skinny with shocking red hair and bright green eyes. She had freckles across her face and arms.

"Hi Kaela, your dad has told me so much about you," she said.

"Hi."

"Niamh is the new publicist for the practice," her father said.

"So I guess tonight is going to be a business meeting?" Kaela asked.

Her father's smile faltered a bit, "No, it's just going to be a nice night out."

Kaela didn't bother answering, she looked over at Amy and held out her hand, "Come on Amy, let's go get dressed."

The two walked off to Kaela's room. Once they got there, Kaela raced to the window and looked out; her father and the woman were still talking. Kaela was not impressed.

For the past few years, her father had gone on a lot of dates but the woman he went out with were either after his money, or too uptight to deal with his daughter and the shadow of his wife. Niamh looked no different.

"Isn't tonight going to be fun?" she mumbled angrily.

Angela typed her ancestor's name into the search engine. She wanted to see what the big deal was. Unfortunately the only websites which came up were capitalism-loving Lord Sabian fans. Angela wasn't really interested in learning how he built his empire up. Frankly, some rich aristocrat coming down to a newly colonised land was not a success story, it was a horror. Gruesome tales were probably hiding in all those websites. Angela shivered and returned to the search engine. Before the page changed, her eyes fell on one website screaming, 'The great crimes of Lord Sabian'. She shivered; that was the exact reason she had never wanted to research him. She erased what she had written into the search engine and wrote, Sabian Family Philanthropist.

Nothing came up.

She scratched her foot and looked at Tesla and Copernicus, the dogs.

"Well, I suppose they weren't really philanthropists. They did make a profit off their land."

The dogs ignored her.

She retyped, Sabian Family Midlands.

More websites than she had expected suddenly popped

onto her screen. She spent the next hour reading through as many as she could.

By the time she had tucked herself into bed that night, she had learnt some interesting information about the people whose blood flowed through her veins.

"So Kaela, your dad tells me that you're very much into horse riding," Niamh said.

The four of them were at Kaela's uncle's vegetarian restaurant, The Sanguine Boat, and this was the first time since they had arrived that Kaela had been brought into the conversation. She looked up at Niamh, the woman had such shocking green eyes – they were almost scary.

"Actually I do little else," Kaela said in her most sickly-sweet voice.

"Yup, it's like she's naked if she is not on a horse," Amy added with a mouthful of bruschetta. This was the first time she had ever experienced the job of building her own meal from the smorgasbord of vegetables, cheeses and sauces on the table. The child had nearly eaten her own weight in veggies.

Both Amy and Niamh had been surprised by this style of eating. Kaela and Leo ate like this every night. It was easy for her, and apparently her father, to forget that others did not.

"That's great. I've always loved horses just never been brave enough to ride," Niamh said.

Kaela smiled at her but didn't say anything.

Niamh had given up on the fried bread and was nibbling the different veg dipped in the cheese sauce, fondue style. This grated Kaela for some reason.

"You should come ride at Apley Towers," Amy said. "Adult classes are on Saturdays."

"Maybe I'll check it out one day," Niamh said with a smile.

Kaela noticed that she had very sharp teeth.

Vampire, she thought.

"Kaela, I love that dress. Where did you get it?" Niamh asked with a toothy smile.

Kaela looked down at her clothing; it was a Chinese dress that she adored wearing, "My dad brought it back from China."

"Pure fluke," Leo said, "I didn't even know if she would like it; it was pink so I bought it. Luckily for me, she likes it."

"Do you like pink?" Niamh asked quite seriously.

"Only if the clothes are pretty."

"I like pink, when I get a horse I'm going to get a pink saddle," Amy said proudly.

From then on the conversation was directed completely at Amy.

Much to Kaela's relief.

Trixie sat in bed that night thinking about what she wanted in a horse. She had always wanted a bright chestnut or pretty palomino, but like most riders at her level, she knew that colour and breed did not matter. The prettiest horse could have the most horrible personality. Just like humans. Kaela had told her to write a list of what she wanted in a horse. Trixie looked down at the list and lifted her eyebrows.

1. Must be fairly well trained at dressage
2. Must ENJOY dressage
3. Must be the same weight and height as Slow-Moe
4. Must get along with every horse in the stable
5. Must have some of my characteristics (funny, charismatic, smart, insanely addictive)
6. Must have no allergies or ailments
7. Must be fairly young
8. Must instinctively hate Bella
9. Must not cost an arm and a leg

"You're not demanding are you?" Trixie said with a sigh.

She threw her notebook aside, switched off her lamp and flopped into bed.

Phoenix: I can't do it Kae.

Angela: You'll be fine.

Kaela: ^^^What she said.

Phoenix: I kept forgetting the course today.

Angela: I find that walking the course beforehand makes it easier to remember it.

Phoenix: Saddles are stupid. You can't feel what the horse is doing.

Angela: That's true.

Kaela: I'm too scared to ride without a saddle.

Phoenix: Really?

Angela: What is a saddle going to do for you?

Kaela: It's safer.

Angela: How?

Kaela leaned back in the chair. She had no answer.

Her father's voice came from the belly of the house. Niamh was still here. It was nearing ten o'clock at night.

Didn't she have a life?

Phoenix: I think it is safer to be bareback.

Angela: In some respects it is.

Phoenix: I can't do this competition.

Angela: Is it because your grandfather just lost? Do you think you will lose too?

Phoenix: Maybe.

Kaela: Maybe you should go to the sweat lodge.

Phoenix: Can't. Too young.

Angela: Make your own then. Or instead, go out riding at sunrise, in the quiet, and decide what you want to do. But I personally think you will be fine. They wouldn't tell you to compete if they didn't think you could do it.

Kaela: Remember, winning is not everything.

Angela: I can attest to that.

Phoenix: What was I thinking by signing up to ride with people who will never understand me?

Kaela: You decided to do something different with your life.

Phoenix: Two roads diverged in the underwood, huh?

Kaela: And you took the one less travelled by.

⊱ Eleven ⊰

"Okay, are you ready to try again?" Wendy asked as Trixie arrived at Apley Towers the next morning.

"Yes, I just hope it's not going to be as disappointing as yesterday."

"It will be if you expect it to be," Wendy said as she buckled two bridles to their reins, "Could you please give these two to Joseph? Thank you."

Trixie took the bridles and slung one over each shoulder as she had been taught all those years ago. She spotted Joseph taking the horses out to the feeding paddock. Sunday was the day off for the equine members of the stables, but there was no rest for the grooms.

"Hi Joe," she said as she caught up with him.

"Beatrix King. My favourite female King," he smiled his toothy grin as he took the bridles and threw them over his own shoulders. "How is horse hunting going?

Should I start preparing a stall?"

"Hardly. I've gotten nowhere. I just can't find the right horse for me."

The words, 'maybe I'm too picky' wanted, desperately, to leave her mouth but wouldn't or couldn't. Trixie ground her teeth against the truth.

"So you are *looking* for a dream horse? You are hoping to *find* the perfect horse?"

"Of course."

Rhapsody put his head out of the stall, a reminder that he needed to be taken to the paddock. Joseph gave the old horse a gentle pat on the neck and tidied his mane, "You know what I have found? When you stop looking to find what you think you want, you end up receiving exactly what you need."

"Are you saying I should stop looking for a horse?" Trixie asked.

"Not at all," Joseph pushed Rhapsody back, opened the door and went into the stall, "I'm saying that once you stop having the image of what it should be, you will find what it *could* be."

He quickly put the halter on Rhapsody and led him out of the stall, "And what it is *meant* to be."

Trixie watched him walk off towards the paddock, "What it could be," she whispered to the wind, "what it is meant to be."

136

Kaela walked into the stable car park but no further. She had her mobile up to her ear and the thought of setting foot near the horses with it terrified her. Her father would kill her if she damaged the stupid little electronic thing. Although, he had been the one to insist that she take it with her today.

Kaela wondered if all men were as generally confused as her father was.

"I told you that they bought all that land."

"They *bought* it from the Dutch and the Zulus though," Angela said.

"Well duh, who else?"

"You don't understand. I always thought my family had robbed people to get their land. The Zulus owned the land, the Dutch colonised the land – a nice way of saying they stole it – and then my family came down with the rest of the British and stole the land from the Dutch."

Kaela shook her head.

"But no, that wasn't it at all. My family bought that land from both Dutch and Zulus. They bought it fair and square. They weren't creeps."

"The complete opposite. They bought it and held onto it to make sure the landscape didn't get ruined. Your family did good, kid. South Africa has national parks because of your ancestors. Be proud."

Angela was quiet for a long time, "I will be," she said finally.

"Our eyes see the present but our hearts see the past," Kaela added.

"Pardon?"

"Something my grandmother always says to me. Her husband was a historian and he had that carved into his desk."

"Our eyes see the present but our hearts see the past," Angela repeated.

Kaela wished her luck for the competition, hung up and went to find Wendy.

The stable was quiet, Sundays were always so calm. Kaela could hear the birds chirping and the monkeys chattering. Those sounds were usually drowned out by the mass amounts of general noise from the stable.

She let herself through the wrought-iron gate and into the pool area. Bart sat on the swing with his mobile in his hand and his bottom lip between his teeth. He pushed himself backwards and then let the swing fall forward. He kept swinging without acknowledging her presence. This only reminded her that she needed to match his stirrup move. Although, the idea of putting her foot into Mouse's stirrup would never work, the horse was far too tall. She would be left hopping on one foot while trying to get the other one in an impossibly high stirrup iron. Kaela was one for physical comedy but there was a time and place for everything, this wasn't one of those times.

Bart still hadn't seen her, he continued to push himself

back and let himself swing forward. Although he had swapped his bottom lip for his left thumbnail.

Kaela watched him in silence. She tried to remember the exact moment she had begun to see him as more than a friend. But she wasn't all that convinced there was one. They had just grown from little kids to bigger kids and then into teens, and she had always found him more interesting than the rest of the people in her life. She could lie and say it had been the day Wendy had had the whole stable over for a Christmas pool party when Kaela was nine. They had all been playing in the pool and the boys were getting a bit too rough with the girls; Bart had rescued her from one of the older riders. Only to dunk her head back under the water once he had seen that she was okay.

It could also have been when she was eleven and he had taught her to spin bowl. To this day, she was the only female cricketer on the stable team. Kaela smiled as she thought of all the times he had taught her something or come to her with history questions. The year before, he had been assigned a part in the school play (much to his incessant horror); he had hated every moment of acting Sebastian in Twelfth Night. But, she had coached him, just as he had coached her with the cricket ball.

"Hello little one," he said without looking up.

He had spotted her. She walked over and sat on the other swing, "What are you busy doing?"

"Nothing. Just going through LetsChat."

"And not putting up any photos," she teased.

He grabbed his mobile, edged his swing closer to hers, put his head next to hers and held the phone in front of their faces.

"Smile."

She did. She also couldn't help but think they looked good together. They matched. His hair a deep brown like her mahogany, both had large blue eyes and both wore soft blue shirts. They looked like a set.

Kaela watched as he put the photo on LetsChat, with the caption, hanging with the fabulous Miss Kae.

"Happy?"

"Yes, you usually make me very happy."

Bart smiled at her and pushed the swing away, "Yes, you too."

Now she had a photo situation to go with her stirrup situation.

What's a girl to do?

Trixie, having found Slow-Moe and given him a loving pat, could see that Wendy was getting ready to leave. She gave the gelding a goodbye kiss and walked over to the cage just behind Wendy's house. This cage was something of a legend at the stable; it was as big as a dining room and had the look of a jungle to it. She could see Bart and Kaela standing inside.

"Hello Trixie," Bart called.

"Hello," Kaela waved.

Trixie waved back and watched them feed Super Dude – Bart's pet tortoise. It was illegal to keep tortoises in South Africa but the Oberon family had inherited this one from the former owners. He had been found – abandoned, thirsty, tired – wandering the property in search of food. A quick visit from a police inspector and vet confirmed Super Dude as ninety-three years young and still going strong. Wendy had been given permission to keep him. While renovating the rest of the stable, she had built this mammoth cage and created the perfect jungle. Two years later, Bart had named him Super Dude and the legend of the Apley tortoise spread far and wide.

Super Dude was grabbing hungrily at the oranges being fed to him. Trixie's eyes fell on Super Dude's shell; he had a gold lightning bolt painted on. The paint glowed in the dark so that Bart could always see him wandering around his mansion of a cage, or for those odd occasions when Super Dude somehow managed to get out of his fortification and took a stroll around the stable. Twice now, Wendy's neighbour had reported a golden ghost *slowly* haunting the stable in the dead of night.

The two fed him the last of the oranges and made their way out of the cage.

"Bye Super Dude, you be super." Bart grinned.

"You've been saying that since you were eight. It's getting old," Kaela said to Bart.

"Bye Super Dude, you be a dude," he corrected.

"Isn't a 'dude' a person who can't ride horses?" Trixie asked.

Kaela and Bart stared at her with wide eyes. She looked from Kaela's blue eyes to Bart's, "What?"

"Are you suggesting that Super Dude should know how to ride?" Kaela asked.

"Of course not," she frowned.

"Good, because I'm not teaching him," Bart said as he led the way to the car, "I would rather teach old man Henry to ride."

"Shuuush," Kaela pointed to the neighbouring house and then glaring at Bart, "he'll hear you."

"Oh please, that crazy old man couldn't hear the fireworks on Bonfire Night. A Roman Candle lit up the place and I saw him on the porch asleep in his rocking chair."

"Either way, you shouldn't be so insulting," Kaela argued.

"Maybe if old man Henry were nicer to us we wouldn't be insulting to him," Trixie added with a glance at the double chimneys on the roof.

"Hey sprogs, are we ready to go?" Wendy called.

Trixie, Bart and Kaela turned away from old man Henry's house and piled into Wendy's car.

"Why do you think the two houses have matching chimneys?" Trixie asked, pointing to the Oberons' house and its neighbour.

"Just the way it was meant to be."

There was that phrase again. Trixie looked out the window as the car reversed. She caught a glimpse of Joseph. Wendy pressed the horn as she passed the grooms, they all raised their hands. All except Joseph. He looked at Trixie and she could hear the words again.

Meant to be.

Their first stop was Equestrian International, a riding academy in the fanciest area of the Midlands.

The shadow of the Drakensburg Mountains fell on them, silencing them. It felt like the land of dragons and old Gods.

No one spoke until they were out of the shadow and in the riding academy.

At Equestrian International, people didn't just ride horses. For them, riding was an art. Some of the most expensive horses in South Africa were stabled there. Not to mention they had many side businesses, one of which was breeding champions and selling them. Of course, these horses cost more than most people's houses. Even the studs that they decided to sell were pricey. And when Equestrian International announced that they were selling Admiral James – one of their most successful studs – the whole world came knocking. The chestnut Thoroughbred was put on display for prospective buyers, and Wendy did not miss the chance to take a good look at him.

"You want to breed Honey with a Thoroughbred?" Kaela asked with a wrinkled nose.

"What's wrong with that?"

"Honey *is* a Thoroughbred!" Kaela exclaimed.

"And?"

"Well, if you breed a Thoroughbred and a Thoroughbred you're going to get a Thoroughbred."

They all looked at her in silence.

"Her deductive reasoning is amazing," Bart teased.

"What's wrong with Thoroughbreds?" Wendy enquired.

"Well, they are like porcelain dolls, pretty to look at but not much good for anything else."

"I'm sure a lot of breeders would disagree with you," Wendy said in a sing-song voice.

"Yeah, breeders maybe. I'm speaking from a rider's perspective. Fergie refuses to jump. Honey refuses everything. DeBurgh will only pay attention to you if your name is preceded by Lord, Lady or Queen. KaPoe would probably be all right if he had a different rider, but now he is not much of a riding horse. The list goes on and on," Kaela said.

Wendy frowned at her, she had clearly never thought of it that way. She went back to inspecting Admiral James, but all of a sudden she looked rather distracted.

◈ Twelve ◈

The Meander Hotel stared back at Trixie with curtained eyes and huge French doors for teeth. It spoke of majesty and mystery, secrets and the past.

This was South Africa's oldest hotel, and at one point, its caretaker had been Terrence King, Trixie's father. The family had lived here while her mother had gone through university. She had also worked in the hotel at night to earn extra money. The two girls had slept on bunk beds squashed into the study of a one-room bungalow on the shores of Lake Rawdon. The bungalow was graciously provided by the hotel in exchange for the low wage they paid her father. It had been a good life. Very little money, but also very few problems. The girls were too young for school and spent their days running wild on the hotel grounds. All the while avoiding the bungalow, as their mother needed to study. The hotel, with its age and grandeur, attracted quite an intriguing guest list. The sisters had learnt to play tennis by watching dukes. They had learnt to play chess by watching presidents challenge prime ministers. They had even run into all manner of celebrities in the dining room, testing the South African food and staring in wonder at the exotic cuisine. But it had all ended before the ink was dry on her mother's degree. Sabrina had been offered a job for a massive trade company in Durban and the family had not looked back – except when they took a moment to remember their sweet little bungalow on the edge of Lake Rawdon.

From what Trixie had heard, the hotel had enlarged it a few years back and refurbished it into a honeymoon cottage.

The Meander Hotel had the added benefit of bordering Equestrian International. When the girls weren't interrupting prestigious guests on holiday, they had climbed through the fence (the same fence Trixie now stood on to stare at her former home), and spent their time helping the grooms. Thanks to their work at Equestrian International, both girls had gone to Apley Towers with knowledge of every aspect of horse riding, except how to ride.

"Trixie."

She turned around and saw Thabo, a teenage groom, walking towards her with two horses in tow.

Thabo had also been a wild child on the Meander hills. His father had worked at Equestrian International, and still did, while his mother worked at the hotel. Unlike Trixie, who had been left to run completely wild, Thabo had been expected to help his father with the horses. He had taught Trixie everything he was expected to know. He now worked at the stables after school and on weekends.

"Hi Thabo," she ran up to him and gave him a hug.

"What you doing on the fence?" he asked.

Trixie looked back at the hotel, "Remembering simpler days, I suppose. Days when my biggest decision was choosing what to wear."

"Oh, it's one of *those* kinds of days."

Trixie laughed and jumped down.

"Okay, so what are you doing at Equestrian International?"

"Wendy's looking at Admiral James," Trixie said with a creased nose.

She had seen Admiral James before and wasn't too interested in him. He was too much of an aristocrat, he had no time or interest in the little people. And so far he had successfully managed to pass that annoying characteristic down to every one of his foals, including Apley's own DeBurgh.

"Oh, she has an audience with His Highness."

"Exactly, and afterwards we're going horse shopping for me," she answered, taking a lead line from him.

"You're getting a horse?" he asked excitedly.

"Yes, a dressage horse. But so far I've looked at one bad horse after another."

"Maybe you're just looking in the wrong places."

"Maybe my standards are just too high."

"Impossible. You're buying the horse aren't you? It has to be right for the horse and the rider to be worth it – and you can *only* do that by having high standards."

Trixie smiled, at least someone was rooting for the other side of the argument.

The two led the horses into the feeding paddock, took off their halters and walked back for more. On the way, Trixie ran into many grooms who wanted to say hi.

"It's just like old times," she said as they finally reached the stables.

"I'll take Dingo, you can take Siren," Thabo said, pointing to the grey in the next stall. Trixie let herself in the stall and stopped dead. The horse in front of her was the funniest looking thing in the world. His ears hung down on his head so it appeared as though he was wearing a hat. His eyes were very far apart, which gave him a cute, goofy look. He appeared to have gotten more food on his face than in his mouth. There were bits of bran mash all over his muzzle as well as in his nostrils, and pieces of hay decorated his face and cheeks. The rest of his body was no better off. The bedding that should have been on the ground was now on his back, and his front legs looked as though he had actually stood in his water bucket.

"Thabo, do you mind if I give this guy a groom before I take him out?"

"Not at all Trixie, not at all. Saves me having to do it."

The tack, as well as grooming equipment, was all secured

in a cupboard outside of every stall. Trixie got the equipment out and started grooming. She did it quickly because she knew the others wouldn't be much longer with Admiral James. It really was just like old times.

Kaela had wandered off on her own too. Shopping for horses that weren't for her was starting to get boring. She wanted to go to the back paddock and play with Equestrian International's Shetland pony.

"Hey, wait up. I'm not fit enough to run after you," Bart called.

She turned to see Bart walking towards her. He was lying of course: not only did he ride on a daily basis but as he was also on his school's swimming team, his arms and legs were muscular and strong, there was no unfit part of him.

"Are the stallions boring you?" she asked.

"Not as much as last night," Bart said when he finally caught up.

"What happened last night?"

"Nothing. My mum was on the phone all night; Björn hung out with his dad, so I was left to entertain myself. There are only so many computer games you can play in one weekend."

"Well, it couldn't have been as bad as my night," Kaela said with a scowl.

"What was so bad about your night?"

"Had dinner with my dad's new girlfriend. And of course she spent the night sucking up to me. 'Oh Kaela I hear you ride', 'oh Kaela that's such a nice dress'. Got kind of irritating," Kaela confessed.

They had reached the back paddock and Midnight, the Shetland pony, came up to them for treats. Kaela stroked his soft face and thought about this new girlfriend. She had to admit there was something different about her. Most girlfriends tried to ignore Kaela. This one was doing the opposite.

"Did she really say she likes your dress?" Bart asked.

Kaela nodded.

"I don't believe it."

"Why not?"

"Because I don't believe that you would wear a dress."

"I only wear this one. It's a very pretty pink dress."

"I like pink on girls, it looks good."

"Did you know that historically pink was a boy's colour? It only changed because of baby clothes made in the 1980s. If we had been born before the 1980s, you would be in pink and I would be in blue."

Bart raised one eyebrow and shook his head, "I would never wear pink simply because it is too much of a bright colour."

"Yeah, I don't think I have ever seen you wear anything but black."

"My school uniform is maroon."

"School uniforms don't count, they are not your choice."

Wendy walked up to them before Bart could answer.

"Should we find your cohort and get out of here before we get mistaken for grooms and put to work?" she asked.

In record time, Trixie had the horse clean and sparkling. As she put the equipment away she saw the plaque denoting his name. Her heart stopped beating. She took a step back in shock.

SIREN'S SONG

"Siren's Song?"

She had to make a conscious effort to breathe, and then felt her mouth smile.

"It's just a coincidence," she said as she clipped a lead line on his halter and led him out of the stall.

Trixie's jaw dropped in utter shock, if Siren had been funny looking in the stall, then he more than made up for it outside. His walk was agile and supple; he held his body in a powerful and responsive stance. He was absolutely beautiful to watch. Trixie stopped walking and Siren stopped next to her. He came to a square halt with his hind legs tucked correctly under his body. If he had been in a dressage ring he would have gotten full marks. Trixie walked on and Siren followed

in his showy stride. Trixie jogged and Siren moved into a trot, it was beautiful – he moved in perfect rhythm and cadence. Trixie was actually sad when she got to the feeding paddock; she would have to let the beautiful horse go.

"You shouldn't have groomed him," Kabelo, another groom and friend of Trixie, said.

"Why not?"

"You'll see."

Trixie took the halter off and gave Siren a light tap on the rump. He sprang into a canter, Trixie expected him to join the herd in the middle of the field, but he cantered past them and made his way to a giant mud puddle probably caused by last night's downpour. As Trixie watched in horror, Siren lay down and rolled in the mud. When his back, stomach and legs were covered in the dirty brown muck, he leaned down and rubbed his face in the mud. Trixie felt like screaming.

"What in the name of Darwin? There is no sun. Why is he covering himself in mud to protect himself when there is no sun?"

"We have no idea," Kabelo said with a smile. "He always rubs himself in mud. If there is no mud, he will make some."

Trixie looked around the feeding paddock: as in all feeding paddocks, there was a lot of shade to protect the horses from the sun, but as in all feeding paddocks, the herds did not gather in it. That was especially bad for greys, who were prone to getting burnt. In the wild, greys and black horses rolled in mud to protect themselves from the

154

sun and to keep cool. Although Trixie was mad that her work had been for nothing, she enjoyed seeing Siren behave as he would in the wild.

"Trixie."

She turned to see Kaela walking towards her.

"I'm coming."

Trixie turned to look at the beautiful grey again; he had made his way to the herd by now. She waved goodbye to the grooms and walked away. She heard a loud whinny and turned to see Siren shaking his mane and approaching the fence.

"I've never seen him do that before," Thabo said.

He whinnied once more then went back to his grazing.

"That's interesting," Trixie said.

"Hi Trixie-True."

"Hi Mom," Trixie said and went to hug her.

"How was horse shopping?" she asked.

"Even worse than yesterday," Trixie moaned.

"So you didn't even see one horse that you liked?"

Trixie hesitated, but then shook her head. An image of Siren slowly crept into her mind, like a long forgotten song: quiet at first, but getting louder the more it was remembered. She pushed it away quickly.

"No, I didn't see any horses I liked." Too bad Siren belonged to Equestrian International and was not for sale.

"Well, just keep looking," her mom said encouragingly.

"I will, the perfect horse is out there."

The song played in her head, soft melodies across her brain that organised to form the picture of Siren.

"I can fetch you from Apley Towers tomorrow afternoon," her mom said as she began dinner.

"Why aren't you working?"

"I am, but I have a meeting with one of our suppliers in Howick and then I'm dropping in at The Meander to say hi to the old crew. I want to see the cottage as well. So I'll be able to pick you up."

Before Trixie knew what she was doing, the words were already out of her mouth.

"I want to come with you."

Her mom turned to look at her in surprise, "You want to come with me to my meeting?"

"No, I want to come with you to The Meander."

"Why?"

She looked disappointed at the prospect of a daughter dragging along to her girls' reunion. Trixie wasn't so sure she wanted to know what they were planning to talk about.

"I want to go to Equestrian International," she quickly said.

"Why?"

"They have horses for sale," Trixie lied.

"You want to miss class? Wouldn't you rather go on Saturday? With Wendy, who knows what she is doing?"

"No, I'd like to go tomorrow please," Trixie said sweetly, "if

I find one I'll talk to Wendy about him or her on Tuesday."

"Okay, just let Wendy know you're not going to be in class."

"Will do," Trixie said with a smile.

The song was almost deafening now, drowning out sense and reason.

She didn't care, she had to follow it.

Kaela Willoughby has been added to a chat with Angela May, Trixie King and Phoenix White Feather.

Kaela could see the little green dot next to Bart's name on her chat list. That small, insignificant green dot signified that he was at Apley right now, sitting in front of his computer, hanging about on LetsChat. Just like the rest of them. How easy it would be to just click on his name and add him to this chat.

Kaela only wished she could.

Phoenix: I did my sunrise ride with Wind Whistler (fell off, landed in slush but that's another story) and I have come to a conclusion.

Angela: Do tell.

Phoenix: I WILL take part.

Kaela: YAY!

Trixie: Woohoooo!!!!

Angela: I'm so happy for you.

Phoenix: BUT …

Kaela: Oh, I love how she throws that in after we have already celebrated.

Angela: But what?

Phoenix: But I want the three of you to do something on the morning I compete. It will be afternoon for you guys already, so you won't have to get up early.

Trixie: What do we need to do?

Phoenix: RIDE!

Kaela: We do that anyway.

Phoenix: No, this is different. I need all of you

158

on horseback sending good vibrations my way. Shared happiness, tripled, and sent to me.

Trixie: We can do an outride.

Angela: We could do it bareback. White Feather style.

Phoenix: I'm riding like you, you are riding like me? What's wrong with this picture?

Kaela's heart thumped against her chest. Quiet Fire was a massive horse, and even though Angela and Phoenix were of the opinion that saddles were not safer, Kaela still believed it was the saddle that kept her safe on Quiet Fire's back. Even if it was simply because it acted as something to grab onto if she needed to. Butterflies fluffed in her stomach, she wasn't so sure she would be joining the bareback brigade.

Phoenix: The competition begins at ten and I only ride just after eleven. So you guys need to figure out what time that is for you.

Angela: Oh that will be simple to calculate.

Trixie: The Lost Kodas will ride together, despite our separate continents and dividing ocean.

❧ Thirteen ❧

"Trixie, what are you doing here again?" Kabelo called.

"Just came to help out while I'm waiting for my mom to finish her meeting," Trixie lied.

She felt guilty about lying so much, but she just had to see Siren again.

"Where are you off to?" Kabelo asked.

"Just gonna walk around."

Trixie made her way to Siren's stall; he was boarded in the school horse section of the stables so he was more than likely going to be ridden in one of the classes. Trixie hoped that he was already in his stall instead of still being at grass.

"You're in luck Trixie, you get to help me groom this monster," Thabo joked as she got to Siren's stall.

"Looks like you're already finished," Trixie said.

Siren's white coat and grey mane were shining with cleanliness and health. But the horse himself did not look too happy; he weaved from side to side as though he had a bad bout of colic.

"Is he okay?" Trixie asked warily.

"Yup, just miserable that he is back in his stall. He's a free spirit; he doesn't like being boxed up."

"Isn't he going to be ridden today?"

"Nope."

"Why not?"

"Nobody to ride him."

"What do you mean?" Trixie asked. *Is Equestrian International lacking riders? Maybe they should reduce their rates.*

"He was bought to be a hunter jumper but he has no interest in the speed that hunter jumpers have to go at. He likes taking things slow. And now he can't be used for any other riding because there are already enough horses. So the poor boy gets boxed up until the owners decide what to do with him."

"Why didn't they check him before they bought him?"

"They bought him from a farm in the south coast, the first time they saw him was when he stepped off the trailer in their car park. They pretty much picked him out of a catalogue and on the catalogue it said that he was a fabulous hunter jumper."

Trixie nodded her understanding; she knew how frustrating it was when people lied just to get the horse sold. It was also heartless. Horses were not inanimate objects.

They were sentient beings with very real feelings. Being treated like furniture was akin to animal abuse.

"So what have they decided to do with him?"

"They haven't decided. They'll probably keep him as beginners' horse; he's got the temperament for it."

Trixie silently screamed. What a waste of talent that would be! Such a well turned out horse handed over to beginners that would ride him at a trot for the rest of his life, and he would never grace the show ring where he so clearly belonged.

"So why don't one of the grooms ride him, just to get rid of some of that pent-up energy?"

"Trixie, there are one hundred and eleven horses here and there are only twenty-eight grooms. We barely have enough time to feed the horses, let alone exercise them as well," Thabo explained. Suddenly he stopped grooming and looked up, "Do you want to ride him today?"

Trixie's mind filled with words. So many words.

Should be.

Could be.

Meant to be.

She shook her head to clear her mind. But all it did was make the words louder.

Stop looking. What was meant to be will come to you.

It will come to you.

It will find you.

What you seek is seeking you!

"Yes," Trixie screamed over the words, "yes, I would love to ride him."

"Go get a hard hat from the equipment room while I tack him, and I'll meet you in front of the dressage square."

Trixie hurried off to the equipment room. The large shed held all the lunging whips, crops, hard hats, and anything else a rider may need to borrow. It appeared as though Equestrian International stocked this room for the advancement of their riders, but Trixie knew that the room was filled with property that had been left over from all the shows the stable hosted – lost property that was never claimed. She quickly found a hat that fit, jammed it on her head and ran out to the square.

There were twelve riding rings, two lunging rings, a dressage square and four warm-up rings at Equestrian International. Riders walked, trotted or cantered in endless circles around the riding rings. The lunging rings held private owners training their new, expensive, mounts. The square was the only one open but Trixie knew that wouldn't be the case for long. She would have to exercise this horse quickly.

Thabo led a fully tacked Siren to the square. Trixie marvelled at this horse. His ears still flopped sideways, making him look like a mad hatter. But the black and yellow studded bridle brought out the brilliance of his eyes. The throat-lash and yellow bit guards brought out the black flecks in his white coat. The same was true of the reins which made the black hairs of his mane shine. The saddle sat on a yellow blanket with 'Siren' engraved in black thread. She stared at him, waiting for that moment where the words would envelope her. But it never came.

Her mind was quiet.

There were no words and no commands and no questions.

Siren silenced her thoughts.

Only the song remained.

His long lashes brushed the air as he looked Trixie up and down. Judging his new rider. Deciding if he was going to make this ride easy or worth it.

"Why is the dressage square open?" Trixie asked.

Thabo handed the reins over and shrugged, "No one doing dressage just yet. That will change soon. Hurry up and mount."

Trixie didn't need to be told twice. She took a deep breath and walked over to Siren's left shoulder. His eye followed her every movement. She put her foot in the stirrup and, with a silent wish to the universe, she pulled herself into the saddle.

The world was better from Siren's saddle. The view of the stable fit perfectly between his ears. The feel of him beneath her made her the queen of existence. She sat up a little straighter and inhaled the scent of the wind. There was something carried within it. Magic and cosmic power.

She felt as though she was where she was meant to be.

Siren gave a little whinny so she gathered up the reins and nudged him into a walk. His gait was smooth, the

gentle rocking from beneath sent her body forwards and backwards. Suddenly there was no Equestrian International. There were no other people and no other horses. There was simply a dressage ring, a row of imaginary judges and Siren.

Trixie put him through a simple dressage test that she had memorised by heart. It was apparent right from the very first aid that Siren had been born to do dressage. He held himself perfectly; he performed his transitions without fault. He danced his way across the dressage square. Siren seemed to understand that they were partners and not a rider dictating to a horse. He understood that it took two of them to make the paces look beautiful. He understood that both horse and rider brought something to the ring and that, of course, was what dressage was all about. Trixie merely had to give the aid, and Siren performed it with excellence. There was a telepathic communication between the two: between her hands and his mouth; her knees and his sides; her body and his. They spoke a language only they could hear.

With an emotion bordering on loss, she sadly brought him to a complete, and correct, halt and saluted the imaginary judges. Loud clapping broke through the silence and filled the air. Trixie, and Siren, turned to look at the source of the noise. It was Shannon Michaels, one of the owners of Equestrian International. A man who had spent her youth yelling at her for being at the stable without a guardian but who wouldn't recognise her now if she paid him.

"That was brilliant," he called out to her.

Trixie walked Siren over to him.

"Do you mind me riding Siren? He desperately needed exercise so I just took the initiative. I hope that's okay," she said nervously. She had been on the receiving end of way too many examples of this man's outrage.

"Not at all, you're being helpful. Have you ridden him before?" Shannon asked politely.

Had he gotten calmer in his old age, or did Trixie's age make her less of a target?

"No, I only met him yesterday." She dismounted so that he did not have to look up at her.

"Well you looked very good. You looked like you and Siren have been riding together for years."

"Thank you," Trixie said shyly, "have you decided what you are going to do with him? I would hate to see such talent going to a beginner rider."

"He can't be ridden by the beginners, he is too big – he's just over fifteen hands. We have decided we're going to cut our losses and sell him," Shannon said with a pat to Siren's neck. "But thanks to you, I see I can sell him as a dressage horse. He looked like he was enjoying himself thoroughly. We'll have to give him a bit more training though, he only has the basics down," Shannon said with a smile.

Trixie's mind was reeling; sell him, a dressage horse, fifteen hands.

"How old is he?"

"Oh he is still a baby, he is only eight," Shannon said. He

frowned at her; she looked like she had just had an epiphany, "Are you okay?"

Trixie nodded, but her mind was not with him. Siren was a dressage horse that was up for sale. He was fifteen hands, the same as Slow-Moe. He weighed the same as Slow-Moe. He was only eight, which meant they would have lots of time together before he would get too old for riding. Trixie had her list memorised off by heart; Siren had already ticked off four of the points. Five if you counted the fact that he was slow and meticulous in his ways, just like Trixie. Sure, he did not have the most training in dressage, but suddenly that didn't seem important any more. She and he could learn together.

"Does he have ailments or allergies?" Trixie asked.

Shannon thought for a moment, "Not that I remember at this moment but if you let me go get his file I will be able to check for you. Why?"

"I think I may know somebody you could sell him to."

Trixie returned Siren to his stall and untacked him. She asked one of the passing grooms to rub him down when he had the chance and then walked to Shannon's office.

"Here is Siren's file," he said, handing her a yellow cardboard folder.

Trixie opened it and scanned the papers. There was a vet's check which stated Siren to be in perfect health and eight years of age. The vet also said that Siren was an Andalusian and 15.3 hands high. The vet's check said nothing else of importance so she skipped to the next page. It was the head groom's report, Trixie knew that when a new horse arrived at most stables, the head groom was given time with the horse in order to establish what kind of temperament the horse had. Trixie read the report.

SIREN'S SONG: Although he could never be a hunter jumper, he is patient and seems to understand his rider. Siren does not like to be pushed to do things. I had to order him to change gaits many times before I learnt that simply asking him politely will get it done. Siren needs a rider whose riding ability is based on partnership rather than obedience. Siren does not want to lead, but will not be lead. He is a calm horse who knows that a walk can take him to the exact same place that a gallop will. He would be perfect for beginners as he will do what he is asked and will never fight them. He is quite a sensitive soul though – he would require a lot of love from the students.

It was signed by the groom. It was useful information, but it would not have mattered if Trixie had never come across it. One ride had taught her all that and more. The next page was a report from the farm on the south coast. It just outlined that Siren had a lot of herd instinct; it was as if he was born and raised in the wild. The report stated that although the herd instincts weren't problematic, they could be trained out of him.

"Barbarians," Trixie muttered. Like Kaela, Trixie always thought it was best to let the horse do what they were born to do. And being in a herd was one of those things.

It carried on to say that as a foal he had a fear of thunder, but he had grown out of that. He still sometimes reacted to a lawn mower if brought too close. He was quite prone to ringworm, having several cases of it a year. But he healed from it very quickly.

Trixie looked up at Shannon who was working with a calculator.

"Isn't ringworm caused by something? It doesn't just happen on its own does it?"

Shannon thought for a moment, "Yes, the horse has to come in contact with the worm, either out in the paddock or from another horse. Why?"

"This report says he has several cases of ringworm a year."

"Then they obviously don't clean their tack properly and the same piece of tack keeps on reinfecting the horse. But some horses just do not have the immune system to battle certain parasites. Siren is probably just highly sensitive to ringworm."

"How would you combat that?" Trixie asked.

"Keep the tack sterilised at all times. Don't let the horse share tack with any other horse. Make sure all paddocks are ringworm free. Maybe have him checked out by the vet quite often. It sounds like a lot of work but prevention is easier than cure," Shannon said.

Trixie nodded and went back to the report. It didn't say anything else of importance. She turned to the last page and her heart stopped beating – it was the receipt for Siren. Equestrian International had paid an arm and a leg and a head for him. He was worth nearly three times what her parents were willing to pay for a horse.

Well that takes him out of the running, Trixie thought sadly.

Just then her mobile rang. Her mother had said she would give Trixie a missed call when she was in the car park. Trixie reluctantly got out of the chair.

"Thank you so much for letting me ride Siren and showing me his records," Trixie said, handing the folder back.

"You're more than welcome. You be sure to tell that person you were thinking of that he is up for sale," Shannon said with a smile.

"Will do," Trixie said sadly.

She ran to her mother's car and hopped in the passenger seat.

Her mother was on the phone, Trixie tried to block out her voice and concentrate on not crying but it was impossible.

After a few minutes, her mother disconnected the call and looked at Trixie, "so, did you see the horses for sale?"

She turned the car on and began reversing.

"*Horse.* Yes I did and he is amazing, he is without a doubt a champion waiting in the wings," Trixie said, almost on the brink of tears.

Her mother stopped reversing, and turned to look at her with big eyes, "So what is the problem? If you like him, take him."

"I can't, Mom," Trixie moaned, the tears finally falling from her eyes, "he costs the same amount as a small house."

Her mother gave a little laugh, "I'm sure he is not that expensive," she said, reaching for a tissue and giving it to her daughter.

"He is, Mom, I saw the receipt. They paid so much for him," she wailed into the tissue.

"Did they buy him to make a profit?" her mother asked.

Trixie was used this way of thinking; her mother wasn't the CEO of a trade company for nothing.

"No, they bought him to win competitions for the stable but the people who sold him to them lied about him. So now they have to cut their losses and sell him as a dressage horse."

Sabrina was quiet for a while, biting on her lip and squinting her eyes. Finally she spoke, "So they actually said that they have to cut their losses?"

"Yes," Trixie whimpered.

"Trix, if somebody says they are going to cut their losses, it means that they are not bothering to make a profit or even break even. They are just trying to recover some of the money they lost."

Trixie slowly took her face out of the sopping tissue and looked at her mother with hope.

"Really?"

"Yes, when we cut our losses we sell our products at a price we know will make sure it leaves the shelves very quickly. Why don't we go talk to these people and find out how much they are selling him for?"

Trixie threw herself into her mother's arms with enough force to knock her backwards, she hit her head on the window and bumped the horn, bringing the attention of everyone in the parking lot – human and horse alike.

"Let's go before we cause a riot," she said.

The two walked hand in hand into Shannon's office.

"Back so soon?" he asked with surprise.

"Yes sir, and we bring good news," Trixie said excitedly.

"I'm always open to hearing good news," he said with a smile.

"We would like to put an offer down on Siren," Sabrina said.

Shannon's eyes grew wide and he stood up quickly, "You want Siren?" he asked in shock.

"Yes, we would like to put an offer down on him," Trixie said, sounding just like her mother.

"Of course, of course," Shannon said breathlessly. "Sit down. Let's discuss it."

Trixie sat down and began discussing a price for the perfect horse, who had somehow found her all on his own.

From: trixie-true@feaguemail.co.za
To: kaelalw2000@feaguemail.co.za; phoenix-wfeather@feaguemail.com; horsecrazyang@feaguemail.co.za
Subject: SERIOUS Horse Win for Team Trixie

Dear kodas

HOLY DARWIN!!!!!!!!!!!!!!!!!!!!!!!!!!!!!!
This horse found me. I didn't find him. He found me.

EVIDENCE TO SUPPORT PREVIOUS CLAIM
1) His name! Duh! Siren's Song! He sang to me. I heard him. He lured me in. I went willingly. I am the sailor to his magical singing voice in the sea.
2) He isn't all that trained in dressage, he can do the basics but wouldn't know the aids for a flying change if they did a song and dance number in front of him. Meaning I stupidly wouldn't have wanted him. But I saw him without riding him, so I could see what the judges would see.
3) If I hadn't have felt so sad and gone to see The Meander, I would never have met him. We would have still been looking at horses.
4) He knew what I wanted and he sang to me. And that day, on the fence, I was quiet enough to hear him.

YOUR REACTIONS WHEN I TOLD YOU THE NEWS

1) Angela: She couldn't be happier for me. She is so looking forward to helping me train him. She thinks it will be so much fun and exciting times lie ahead.

2) Kaela: "Why is he named after a mermaid?"

ME: "He is not named after a mermaid. A Siren is a bird with a woman's face. Don't you know anything about Greek mythology?"

Kaela: "If they are birds, why are they in the sea?"

ME: "They are seabirds."

Kaela: "What in the name of Pan is a seabird?"

ME: "A bird that lives in the sea."

Kaela: "That's a fish."

ME: "No In Greek mythology it's a powerful woman, with the body of a bird and the face of a human."

Kaela: "So why on earth is it living in the sea?" (By this point, I gave up.)

3) Phoenix: "He is named after Greek Mythology! Just like my brothers and me! I love it! He was destined to be part of the kodas." (At this point Kaela interrupted to remind everyone that Phoenix was the only koda named after Greek mythology.)

CONCLUSION

I HAVE A HORSE!!! AND HE IS PERFECT IN EV-
ERY WAY!!! WE ARE GOING TO LEARN DRES-
SAGE TOGETHER AND I CAN'T WAIT!!!

❧ Fourteen ❧

Trixie cycled into Apley Towers with a giant grin moulded on her face. Equestrian International would be delivering Siren in an hour's time and she could not wait. She looked around the stable before parking her bike. She could see a mahogany-haired girl teaching the beginners' class. Trixie frowned at her, for some odd reason Kaela was wearing a very pretty and flattering pink top.

Pink? That's odd, Trixie thought with a laugh.

Kaela was something of a tomboy, never bothering with looks or outfits, and here she was standing in black jodhpurs and a cute little pink top with her hair neatly French plaited.

"That's very odd," Trixie said and shook her head.

She looked to the other side of the stables where Angela was jumping Dawn in and out of the feeding paddock in a tighter circle each time. Strangely, Angela – who usually wore the pretty tops – wore a black oversized man's t-shirt.

"They've swapped! I'm in a Twilight Zone."

"Vindicated!"

Trixie turned to look at Russell who stood mumbling to himself as he typed something into his mobile, "Vindicated?"

"Yes, I am no longer a criminal."

"I wasn't aware you were a criminal," Trixie said with a cautious step backwards.

"Yeah, on Saturday I took my library books back. They claimed I had left one at home. I claimed I hadn't. I went home. I searched."

"Did you find it?"

Russell bit his bottom lip and shook his head, "Nope, wasn't at home. Yet they claimed it wasn't at the library. But I knew I was being swindled, you know?"

"No."

"So I went back to the library today and guess what I found on the shelf."

Trixie shook her head and took another step back.

"The book! They had it the whole time. It's a conspiracy."

Trixie chuckled, "The great detective Russell A. Drover unravels yet another earth-shattering conspiracy."

Russell put his arms on his hips and nodded, "Lesser men would have caved but not me."

"And to think," Trixie added with her own shake of the head, "that library would have gotten away with it."

"I know, but somebody had to stop them from making money somehow."

"And exploiting the public's right to read."

"It's a tough job but someone has to do it."

Trixie sighed and shook her head sadly, "What would the shire do without you?"

Russell shrugged, "Probably have to dig up Sherlock Holmes."

Trixie smiled at the joker. Russell made her laugh and brightened her days when he momentarily forgot that he was meant to be flirting or acting cool or in any way trying to get her attention. It reminded her of years gone by, when she and Russell would spend their afternoons joking and things were easy.

Now nothing was ever easy.

Trixie resented this crush. It had ruined their friendship.

She looked over at Angela hoping that Russell would take the hint to leave before he said something that would ruin this moment. Out of the corner of her eye she could see him looking in the same direction with a wrinkled nose.

"Hey, why is Angela wearing my shirt?" he flustered off to investigate.

Trixie, glad for the distraction, parked her bike and walked over to the stables. Wendy said she could pick any of the open stables, but she had better hurry because they weren't going to be open for very long. From that statement, Trixie could guess that Wendy had finally found her perfect stallion.

"So when's the new arrival getting here?" a voice asked.

Trixie turned to see Bart riding Mouse; he looked like he was going to ride him right into the stall.

"In an hour," Trixie said breathlessly, she still could not believe that she owned her own horse. Well, technically her parents owned Siren, but in spirit, he was all hers.

"I can see how excited you are, you're doing some sort of jig there," he said, pointing to her feet.

Trixie looked down to see that she was indeed doing a mini jig. It looked extremely funny in the big horse riding boots.

"I am excited," she exclaimed, then she looked at Mouse. He was sweating quite heavily. As a matter of fact, so was Bart. "Did you have a hectic workout or something?"

"I'm getting Mouse in shape, he's been slacking lately," Bart explained as he dismounted.

Trixie noticed that his legs were a bit shaky on solid ground and he seemed to lean on Mouse for a split second before taking his first step.

"Looks like you had a bit of a workout too," Trixie said with a frown.

Bart gave a quick laugh, flashing his dimple Trixie's way, "I have to say, I haven't worked that hard on a horse in a while."

"So why are you pushing yourself, and Mouse, so hard?"

"I'm getting us ready for Equestrian International's Showing Season," he explained as he began untacking.

"You're taking part?" Trixie asked with interest.

Bart only pleasure rode, he never took part in any show unless it took place at Apley Towers. He especially never took part in any of Equestrian International's shows, and here he was saying that he wanted to be ready for the Season, which meant a show every second weekend for four months.

"Yup."

"Why are you taking part in the Season?"

"My mother is still trying to get interest in Apley Towers and she wants me to compete," Bart said tiredly, he and Mouse were both half-asleep.

Trixie nodded her understanding – the stables which housed the winners always got attention. And Bart was just a naturally good rider, no doubt inheriting it from his mother and his grandparents, who had been international show jumpers in their youth. So it was almost guaranteed that, with practice, Bart would win. But what was in it for him?

"What do you get out of it?" Trixie asked slyly.

"You don't believe that I would do something out of the kindness of my heart?"

"Nope, you're a teenager – we don't do that," Trixie said, "or, at least, we don't let anyone know we do that."

"Well spotted," Bart said with a smile, "I get to keep the prize money if there is any. And ..." Bart trailed off.

"And?" Trixie asked.

Suddenly Bart was quite elusive; he had ducked behind Mouse and hadn't emerged.

"Okay, fine, I get it. Something in it for you but you don't really want to talk about it."

"Right now it is a dream that hasn't gotten off the ground and might not even," he said quietly.

"What's the dream?"

He peeped around Mouse's neck and shook his head.

Trixie smiled, "Will you ever tell us?"

"Yes, just let me get more of a handle on this dream first."

Trixie nodded, "As long as the dream is worth it."

"Right now, it is not worth it," Bart said as he hobbled to the door.

"Well I have faith in you," Trixie said with a smile.

Just then she heard a horsebox enter the premises. She turned and galloped to the car park, leaving behind her a confused Bart calling, "What's up with Kaela's pink top?" but Trixie wasn't sticking around to answer. The car leading the horsebox did not say Equestrian International on the side; it said *Twickenham Stables* in bright purple letters.

"Hi," a man said as he climbed out.

"Hi," Trixie said.

"We got the stallion. We call him number twenty-seven, I'm not sure what you'd like to call him," the man said with a giant smile. Trixie thought he looked slightly familiar.

"Hi," Wendy called as she jogged into the car park, "I wasn't expecting you for a while."

"Traffic wasn't that bad," he said with another smile.

Next came Kaela. She ran into the car park and stood

breathlessly for a second before declaring, "What stallion did you buy? I knew you were going to buy one from them, I could just feel it."

"Do we know this man?" Trixie whispered.

"Yes, we went to his farm on Saturday."

Trixie just nodded, the weekend was one gigantic blur; she couldn't have remembered this man if she tried.

"Well Kaela, why don't you go take a look at the stallion?" he said.

"Thank you Michael, I would love to," she said with a naughty smile, and whispered quickly to Trixie, "I know why *he* came to deliver it."

Trixie frowned. *Why?*

The girls went around the horsebox to look at the stallion. Kaela's eyes widened in amazement as she saw the horse.

"It's the Kladruber!" she exclaimed.

"Have we met this horse?" Trixie asked.

"Yes, we met him on Saturday. This horse has the most amazing spirit. He's like nothing I've ever seen before," Kaela said with excitement as she grabbed Trixie's arm and squeezed.

"Well then maybe you'd like to lead him to the stable?" Michael asked as he walked up behind them.

"I would love to," Kaela sighed.

Michael led the stallion down the ramp and handed the lead rope to Kaela.

"Walk in front of him," Michael said.

"Are you crazy?" Kaela asked. The stallion was so big that Kaela could easily walk under his head without ducking. "If I walk in front of him, he will crush me if he bolts."

Michael smiled and shook his head, "That's just it, he won't bolt if you walk in front of him. In the wild the alpha horse walks directly in front of his herd for protection. Number twenty-seven was brought up to feel safe and confident if somebody walks in front of him. He looks to you for protection."

Kaela looked at the seventeen hands high jet-black Spanish horse and slowly walked in front of him. He followed her without a problem, even stretching his neck to sniff her hair. He nodded, as if deciding she was there for protection, and returned to staring curiously at Apley Towers. Kaela led him to the first empty stall. She unclipped his halter, gave him a few strokes along his velvety face and returned to the car park.

"Did you enjoy that?" Michael asked.

"It was amazing; it was as though I didn't even need a halter and lead line. It was like he would just follow me because I was in front," she said elatedly.

"You see, stallions are not that bad huh?" he asked with a cheeky smile.

Kaela shook her head; she was starting to like this guy and judging from Wendy's body language, she wasn't the only one.

Half an hour later, Michael left. Wendy went to see to

the stallion and Kaela followed her. Trixie couldn't help but think that she had definitely missed something. Wendy had bought a stallion but seemed to be more interested in the breeder than the horse. Kaela and the breeder seemed to be very good friends for some reason. But the strangest thing of all, Kaela was dressed up quite prettily today. Come to think of it, so was Wendy.

"What's going on?" Trixie asked the air.

But before the air had time to answer, a second horsebox entered Apley Towers. Trixie almost jumped out of her skin until she saw who was driving. It was the cowboy with the gold tooth.

"Tracey, right?" he said as he jumped out.

"Trixie," she said with more force than she intended to.

"Trixie, right, right. Well, she's here."

Trixie went around the horsebox and was greeted with a strawberry rump.

"Sea Coral?"

"Yup, I was so happy when you decided to take her. She's some horse."

"But –"

Trixie was interrupted by Wendy.

"Winnie, hi, I made it."

"Hi," Wendy said without correcting him, "how is she?"

"She's fine; she's a good horse."

"Great."

Wendy let herself into the horsebox and led Sea Coral

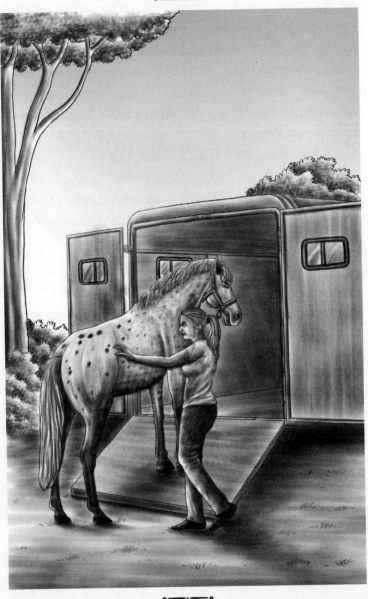

out herself. The cowboy followed her down the path to the stables.

"What is going on here?" Trixie asked loudly.

But before there could be an answer, Equestrian International's horse trailer drove into the car park. Thabo was driving; he jumped out and gave Trixie a hug.

"I'm so glad Siren's going to the best owner in the world," he said excitedly.

The two got Siren out of the trailer without hassle. Thabo went back to fetch everything that belonged to the horse. Trixie remembered what Michael had said about herd instinct and the alpha male. She also remembered what Siren's reports had said about him being led by his herd instincts. She stepped in front of him and led him that way. He also stretched his neck and sniffed at her head. She turned in time to see him nod.

Trixie led Siren to the stall between Mouse and Sea Coral. He greeted each horse in turn. She giggled as she remembered her list that stipulated that the horse had to get along with other horses.

Once all three new horses were settled in, the humans were free to make their way to the ring where Derrick was already halfway through teaching the intermediates.

"Okay," Kaela said, "why did you buy the Kladruber?"

"Because, like you said, he has a spirit you have never seen in any other horse before. I'm hoping he passes that beautiful characteristic down," Wendy answered.

"What are you going to name him?" Kaela asked.

"You've already named him."

"I have?"

Wendy nodded with a sly smile on her face.

"Spirit?" Kaela asked gently.

Wendy nodded again.

"Good name," Kaela said proudly.

"Why did you buy Sea Coral?" Trixie asked.

"Two horses for the price of one? That's a bargain," Wendy said with a smile.

"So you went out to buy one horse and you bought three?" Angela asked as she joined them at the table, "you're such a typical woman."

"Speaking of being a woman," Trixie said to Kaela, "what's with the pretty top?"

Kaela looked down at her pink shirt and smiled, "Some woman that is trying to win my father over bought it for me. Normally I refuse presents from his would-be girlfriends, but the top was just so nice I couldn't resist. If she asks, I used it as a saddle rag."

"And you?" Trixie turned on Angela, "Why are you wearing Russell's shirt?"

Kaela and Wendy both raised their eyebrows at this news. Trixie felt a small kick in her gut.

Why was Angela wearing Russell's shirt?

"Are we missing something?" Kaela asked.

"Yes, is there a new stable romance I am unaware of?"

Angela shook her head, "No of course not. I didn't even have his permission. All that happened was that Dawn was kind enough to let me take the jump without her. I flew over her head and directly in a huge mud puddle. See?" she grabbed her blonde ponytail and showed the mud streaking through it. "My shirt was soaked with mud and it was cold and uncomfortable, but I didn't have a spare one. Joseph told me that Russell had left his shirt here and I should wear that and just explain my predicament."

"And did you?"

"Of course, I'm wearing it right now."

"No," Kaela shook her head, tendrils of gleaming brown hair came loose from the plait and framed her face, "I mean, did you explain the predicament?"

"Yes, he was quite excited to have a woman wearing his clothes," Angela said with a shrug.

Wendy and Kaela laughed loudly. Trixie smiled with thin lips. She didn't find it funny. She found it rude that Angela had just helped herself to Russell's shirt. After all, that was Russell's property. No woman should be wearing it.

"Next time that happens, Angela, let me know and you can borrow one of Bart's shirts," Wendy said.

Kaela instantly stopped laughing and sat quietly looking at Wendy with thin, white lips. *That* made Trixie laugh.

"Someone is calling you," Angela said and gestured towards the stable.

Trixie heard a gentle whinny; she glanced over and saw

189

Siren looking her way. She walked over to him and rubbed his velvet nose.

"Hey boy, do you like your new home?" she asked quietly.

He closed his eyes and breathed onto her hand, a sign that he accepted her as a friend.

She leaned her head on his, closed her eyes and just relaxed against him.

They stayed like that for a few minutes, horse and rider pressed head to head, enjoying one another's company.

Eventually Trixie whispered what had been on her mind all day.

"I'm so glad I found you, it was meant to be."

Kaela took a deep breath. Time to match Bart's stirrup trick.

She stopped outside the wrought iron gate and took her boots, socks and chaps off. Then she walked into the pool area. Bart, in the midst of a butterfly stroke lap, didn't see her. She walked into the gazebo, threw her riding gear down and stripped off her jodhpurs and t-shirt until she was wearing only her 1950s-style blue swimming costume. Bart still hadn't seen her.

She took one last breath and walked over to the small white diving board. She carefully walked to the edge and waited for him to spot her.

Bart did one last lap and then came up for air. He had his back to her. She watched as he took a few minutes to calm his heart rate and breathing. He then took his goggles off and tossed them on the grass.

She waited with bated breath for him to turn around.

When he eventually did, he jumped at the sight of her and stood up quickly.

She smiled and said, "Did you ever notice that no one watches anyone else when you are around? All eyes are on you. You set the stage alight."

And with that she jumped in the pool, swam over and dunked his head under the water.

✧ Fifteen ✧

Kaela loosened her grip on Dawn's mane. Her legs were strong. They held her in place. She cantered with more ease than she ever did with a saddle.

Phoenix and Angela had been right. A saddle disrupted the rider's ability to communicate with the horse.

Although, she wouldn't dare try to jump without a saddle.

She looked across the area known as Shaded Vale. It was open: green fields in the Midlands, surrounded on every side by a cloudless, soft blue sky.

Angela's father had received special permission from the owner for the girls to ride across his land. Mr May had then carted Fergie, Dawn and Siren to Shaded Vale in his father's horsebox.

Angela rode Fergie and had twice taken off at such a fast gallop that the other two hadn't even bothered to try to keep up. Angela had been born to ride. She had no saddle and still barely moved from her position despite the pounding of the horse beneath her. How she kept her legs so still was beyond Kaela.

Angela was magic on a horse.

Kaela felt an odd peace in the Midlands, as though time stood still. There was something old and hidden in this world. It felt to Kaela as though she stood in the cradle of mankind. Had the first ever chimpanzee decided to stand up straight for the first time right where she and Dawn stood? Did humanity begin in the quiet world which bordered the mighty Drakensburg Mountains?

It felt like it.

She closed her eyes, breathed in the power and energy of the land, became the history of mankind and imagined that lightness flowing straight into Phoenix.

"Good luck my friend," she whispered.

Angela, feeling restless and transient, kicked Fergie into a gallop whenever the ground looked sturdy enough. This was the land that her ancestors had found and bought.

They had not stolen it in an era of colonisation. They had not fought uneven and unfair wars for it. They had not committed crimes in order to take it like she had always thought.

They had bought it, fair and square.

And they had bought it, not for profit, but in order to keep it as it always was. They had preserved the land for future generations.

For her.

Tears stung her eyes as she looked at the endless green land that had been saved. The hills and crags, streams and woods and finally, the Dragon Mountains, with their eternal mist and crashing sounds of hundreds of waterfalls.

What had her ancestors felt when they had been here, maybe even on horseback, and looked at this beautiful land?

She closed her eyes and imagined herself as Lady Sabian (in some ways she already was), having the power to save this land from anything that threatened it.

She imagined that power as a bridge and sent it to Phoenix.

"Good luck, Lady White Feather!"

Trixie trotted Siren in a serpentine. She wanted to see how much he knew and where she would have to start working with him.

It suddenly didn't seem so important to move forward in dressage as quickly as possible. Suddenly, working with Siren at his own pace seemed to be the most exciting prospect in the world.

Siren seemed to enjoy this challenge of doing something

he had never tried before. Trixie let go of the reins and directed him with her legs. Although she didn't really need to, Siren was more than happy to continue in his serpentine motion. She spread her arms out like wings and felt as though she were flying. The wind through her hair and her closed eyes felt more freeing than anything she had ever done before.

She held that freedom close to her heart and sent it to Phoenix.

"Good luck," she whispered.

She nearly fell over Siren's head when he suddenly came to a stop. She had no saddle to grip onto and having her arms spread out like a human bird had put her in a rather dangerous position. She smiled sheepishly at Siren's neck.

"Yes, I get it, my boy. I get it. Riding is not to be taken lightly. You are absolutely right. I promise you that I will always take it seriously and together we will always be safe and okay. I'll take care of you and you take care of me."

He gave a gentle nicker.

"I agree, Siren. Let's ride the back of the wind."

She gave him a nudge and he sprang into a gallop.

She pushed herself low on his neck and used her legs to grip as tightly as she could.

Soon both Kaela and Angela joined her.

The girls galloped across the land, through the stream and down the hill, stopping only when they reached the rocks of the Dragon Mountains.

There they stood in humble silence in the shadow of the mountains.

LetsChat: Sunday 16 March

Kalea Willoughby: *To our dear friend, Phoenix White Feather. May our good vibes as we ride in the Midlands fly over our continent, over the ocean and into your heart. But may you remember that winning isn't everything. Just competing, just facing your fears, is the greatest achievement of all. Good luck. We are with you in spirit. Love, The Lost Kodas.*

Bart Oberon: *"Who could refrain that had a heart to love and in that heart, courage to make love known?"*
William Shakespeare

Angela May: *I am SO proud to be part of the Sabian family!!!!*

Trixie King: *What you seek is seeking you! Just have a little trust and pixie dust!*

Phoenix White Feather: *I got a ribbon. It says CLEAR ROUND on the streamers. It is given to those who did not place anywhere, but made it through the course with no faults. Just a game prize for those did not receive the real ribbons. Just a token to show that you had competed (but had ultimately achieved nothing more than that). At the end of the day, nothing more than a second-class trinket to show that I have placed nowhere.*

OR, a ribbon to show that I have conquered my fears!!!!

A token to show that, like my name, I have risen from the ashes, tried something new (no matter how scary), and have opened new doors and created new beginnings.

A CLEAR ROUND ribbon: probably the most precious I will ever receive.

Hera White Feather: *I'm so proud of you. Watching you ride with a saddle in a course just like in the Empire Games was amazing. I'm so glad I bunked work to see you. I couldn't be prouder to have you as a daughter.*

Phoenix White Feather: *I am the Phoenix, I rose from the ashes and I took the road less travelled and that has made all the difference.*

Satyr White Feather: *I am the Satyr, can I borrow five bucks?*

An interview with Myra King

Where did your main inspiration for Apley Towers come from?

From my own adventures with my riding friends and our stable. Most of what Kaela gets up to, I did at one point in my life.

Did you ride horses when you were a child? Do you still ride now?

I rode for most of my childhood, both in lessons and pleasure riding with friends. I don't ride anymore as I had a serious fall ten years ago and now it is painful to sit in a saddle for a long time.

Did you have a favourite horse when you were younger? Why?

The first horse to show me attitude was a gelding named Pumbaa, but he also rescued me from what would have been a very sticky situation. He was one of the horses to make a massive impact in my life. Quiet Fire was the horse I rode most in lessons and I fell in love with him from the very first moment I laid eyes on him. He was black and beautiful, and carried me as though I was royalty. It was easy to imagine myself in a fantasy novel on his back. Another adorable horse who I'll never forget is a gelding named Jinky. He was a former champion but retired at our stable and was the first horse I ever jumped with. He taught me to fly.

What has been your best riding experience, and your scariest riding experience?

My best riding experience was riding on the beach in Mexico. I love Native American culture and being able to ride on their beach with the tribe, the way they ride, was magic. My scariest riding experience was when I was eleven and I started riding more advanced horses. The jump was put up to 1m, which I had never jumped before, and the horse bolted forward before I was ready. I lost my stirrups and he was cantering far quicker than I was used to so I nearly fell out of the saddle. I had to grip really tightly with my calves. But it was the first time that a horse had to literally launch himself to get over the jump so it was the first time I was aware of the fact that the horse was flying through the air with me on top of him. I had to grip his neck just to stay on, which means I didn't have my reins to stop him. I ended up having to throw myself off to get myself to safety. I must have accidentally told the horse to turn right though, because as soon as I fell, he turned and I landed up underneath him and he had to jump over me. I still have the scar from where his hoof cut me.

What was it like growing up and riding in South Africa?
It was great to have hot weather for most of the year. Our riding lessons were always done in beautiful sunshine and around lots of nature. The thing I enjoyed most about South Africa was the animals. I grew up with the ability to see elephants, lions and leopards in the wild. I can't say I miss the monkeys though; I was always scared of them. They frequently broke into my house and stole my soap.

How do you come up with all of the different characters in the books?
Some of the characters are based on my friends. A lot of the characters are different facets of my own personality. But a few of them came to me on their own.

Do you have any strange writing habits?
I sometimes have to walk around speaking the character's dialogue out loud. The neighbors know me as the mad writer who holds entire conversations with herself.

Do you have any tips or advice for aspiring writers?
Pay close attention to the world and write about it as much as you can.

Do you have any plans to write more books after Apley Towers?
I'm always writing something.

A sneak preview from book four in the *Apley Towers* series

APLEY TOWERS

Restless Warrior

❧ One ❧

The firelight flickered across his eyes. He was shy. It was an endearing quality.

It made her smile.

He could look into her eyes for only a few seconds before smiling and looking away. He didn't look away for long. His eyes found hers just as quickly as they had left them.

The fire wasn't truly needed. It was a warmish April night in South Africa and the land still held the heat from the sun. It pulsed around the wooden house like a heartbeat in love. Lions called to their queens in the still of the savannah. If you listened closely, there was a gentle thump as each elephant in the herd put his heavy foot on the soft red sand.

Kaela smiled at the sound of Africa.

Bart smiled back and took a sip from the tin cup in his hand.

"Can I tell you a secret?" he whispered.

"Of course."

"I feel…"

"Kaela! Earth to Kaela! Hello Space Cowgirl, anybody there?"

Kaela Willoughby quickly snapped out of her daydream and focused on the face in front of her. It was Trixie King, her best friend. The two girls were on a school field trip at the local museum. Kaela's over-active imagination had run rampant when the students had arrived at the hundred year old photos. She had seen a photograph of an old Voortrekker couple standing in front of their house. Kaela had liked the dress and before she knew it, it was herself in the photo, standing in the arms of a boy she did not have the courage to tell her secrets too.

"I wonder if you could take photos like this," Trixie said, "That camera does have the option to take the photo in black and white."

"This is sepia," Kaela explained, "it's shades of brown."

"Whatever. Do you think your camera could take photos like this?"

Trixie was referring to the really expensive and gadget-happy camera that Kaela had been given. It had enough buttons to resemble a space shuttle; every time Kaela pressed one she half expected to land on Jupiter.

"It could take photos in sepia but it's not going to look like this. It'll look like a photo taken with the sepia application activated," Kaela said.

"Who gave the camera to you?" Tessigan Brailyn asked.

Tess, the editor in chief at the High School newspaper, fancied herself as something of a camera expert. She had nearly fainted when Kaela had shown the space rocket apparatus to her.

"Niamh – my dad's new girlfriend - gave it to me. She got a new one so she gave her old one to me," Kaela said.

"So she is officially your dad's girlfriend now?" Tess asked.

Kaela shrugged, "That's how he introduced her to his friend a few days ago. So I guess."

"Are we okay with this?"

Kaela shrugged, "Not much I can do about it, is there?"

"Is she nice?"

"Yes," Trixie answered for her.

Kaela shrugged again, "She's all right. I can't complain."

I just don't want her to replace my mother in my father's eyes, she thought.

"Man, this museum is boring," Trixie said.

"Maybe I could liven things up a bit," Kaela suggested.

"How?"

Kaela looked around the museum. It was a large building dedicated to the history of their home town, Port St. Christopher. Although, it only ever seemed to speak of the boring bits of history. Kaela's grandfather had been a historian and his constant facts and years and names drove a person batty. The family avoided his history talks on general principle, except at Christmas. After one or two glasses of mulled wine, the man started harking on about the gross and funny bits of history. Kaela tried to remember all that he had told them.

A photo of the South African soldiers sent to fight on the side of Mother England during World War One hung above a rack of medals.

Kaela raced to the front of the class, put her hands behind her back and cleared her throat loudly, "Ladies and Gentlemen," the class looked at her, "If you will look towards this photo of the South African soldiers at Port St. Christopher harbour, you will notice the heavy kitbags they are carrying. One of the items packed deep within those bags was jars of strawberry jam. Highly prized in the trenches. It was gold to the hungry soldiers. But once the jam was finished - which happened surprisingly quickly - the jar was gold too."

"What did they do with it?" Trixie called.

"They filled the empty jars with explosives and hurled them over the top of the trench into No Man's Land. The Germans quickly caught onto this and did the same. There was only one difference between the German trenches and the British trenches."

"What was that?" someone called.

Kaela turned and faced the photo, she pointed to something standing between the legs of two mischievous looking soldiers, "That."

"What is it?"

"A cricket bat."

"How did that help?"

"Germans didn't play cricket. Britain, South Africa, New Zealand and Australia did."

"So?"

"So . . . When the Germans threw their jam jars, these South African soldiers would have grabbed that bat and knocked the jam jar straight back out. Boomerang bombs."

"Just the South African soldiers?"

"Of course not. Every soldier in the British trench could play cricket."

The class clapped. Kaela did a bow.

"Tell us more," one of the boys cried.

Kaela looked around the room, trying to remember what else her grandfather had said. She should really have given him more mulled wine. Her eyes fell on a ship at harbour. She raced across the room with twenty fourteen year olds on her tail.

"This ship is called The Waratah. It sailed from our harbour in 1908 with 221 passengers and was never seen again."

"It sank?"

Kaela lifted her arms and shrugged her shoulders, "We don't know."

"How can you not know?"

"Who's 'we'?" Trixie teased.

"The ship was coming from Australia, it stopped here to let off two passengers, it then sailed out to sea with a plan to stop at Cape Town but never made it there. In 1908 there was all sorts of ways of communicating with the mainland, if there was something wrong they would have been able to tell someone. But they didn't. They just did not arrive in Cape Town."

"What are the theories?" Mr Keen, her history teacher asked.

Kaela did not fail to notice that the history teacher had just asked her opinion on history.

"Well, it could have been a rogue wave. They are extremely common around the coast of South Africa. During the Tudor and Stuart eras, nearly every ship that sailed around the coast was sunk by a rogue wave. The only difference is that those ships were wooden and a lot smaller, so a lot easier to sink. A rogue wave may have just rolled The Waratah and not sunk it. It could also have been an explosion in the coal room. But then why didn't they let anyone know they were on fire? Why didn't they get people off?"

The class quietly stared at the painting.

Finally, Kaela could stand it no longer, "Why is no one asking me why those people got off the ship at our harbour?"

The class looked at her with wide eyes.

"Why?" Mr Keen asked.

"Because the one man had a dream that ship would sink and kill everyone on it."

Silence.

Just like around the Christmas table when her grandfather had said that exact thing.

"But, then that just proves that the ship just sank," a girl said.

Kaela smiled and answered the exact way her grandfather had, "If that is the case, why haven't they found the ship on the ocean floor? They have found the Titanic, why haven't they found The Waratah?"

The Grade Nine students stared at Kaela with wide eyes and ashen faces. Trixie, who knew this story, began clapping and whooping.

"More, more," she cried.

Like a Ghost of Christmas Past, her grandfather's voice filled her brain and pointed to exhibits and photos she had missed, screaming facts she had thought she had forgotten.

Reminding her of the love of history he had instilled in her.

And her long lost mother.

It was something they both shared.

Angela May marched along the beaten path of her family's sugarcane field. She mumbled angrily to herself as she stomped along. Her mother, a scientist and lecturer, home-schooled Angela and expected nothing but the best from her daughter. As much as Angela excelled in nearly every subject she was taught, science eluded her. The words and their incomprehensible meanings made her head want to explode. If HE is helium and H is hydrogen, why in Darwin's name is K potassium or FE iron? She was utterly convinced that scientists rolled out of bed in the morning with the intent to torture humanity. Why name it Toxicodendron Vernix, when it is essentially just a poisonous leaf? Would it not make more sense to name it Poison Leaf instead? Scientists got together in their little groups and planned how to confuse everyone else. She was sure of it.

Her mother had sent her out to walk to help her memorise the periodic table. Why on earth she would need to know that thing was beyond her. But she had learned long ago not to cross her mother. Especially when it came to science.

She took the paper out of her pocket and re-read all the pointless nicknames for the elements.

"AU is gold and AG is silver," she read out loud, "Why not just say gold or silver? How much time did you people waste coming up with these stupid nicknames?"

Probably none at all, they probably all got together for dinner and said, "What are the letters which do not appear in the words gold or silver, we'll use those as the key".

Suddenly Angela wasn't the only one in the sugarcane who was stomping. The ground literally vibrated beneath her feet. She looked up to see four elephants walking across the path. The dogs put their tails between their legs and ran back home.

Angela watched the bull and his three cows lumber across the path and into the sugarcane. It looked like one of the cows was pregnant. Angela stayed as still as possible. The last thing she needed was for this bull elephant to see her as a threat to the unborn calf. They were far down the path but there would be no way on earth that Angela would get to safety before he caught up to her.

The autumn sun shone behind the elephants and the cool breeze that blew through the sugarcane gave Angela goosebumps, the good kind. She sat and watched the marvels of nature as they walked back through the fields. The national park bordered her family land, the elephants must have broken the fence and come into the fields for a day out. They headed back home with not a care in the world.

"Bye ellies," Angela whispered.

Apparently the bull heard her, he stopped and turned to stare. Angela's heart beat in her throat. He shook his big ears, waved his trunk and walked off.

He had said goodbye too.

"If you mention that show one more time I am going to run down the road screaming my head off."

Trixie rolled her eyes, "You are such a diva. That show is brilliant. The whole world agrees. You are the only one who doesn't like it."

"I am the only one who seems to realise how factually incorrect it is," Kaela said.

"Oh facts-schmacks. What do facts matter in entertainment?"

"Surprisingly little, apparently."

The girls boarded the school bus and took a seat towards the middle. Trixie wasn't sure where this positioning put them on the social ladder. They weren't up in front with the teacher's pets but weren't in the back with the popular kids. Looking around, Trixie decided that the middle of the bus was for the teenagers who refused to adhere to any labels or social rules.

The bus ride back from a field trip was always disappointing. Especially when the bus would return nearly an hour before school ended. What were you meant to do with that time? Sit at the desk and stare at the clock? Plan a revolution?

"Can you believe the Season at Equestrian International starts in a few weeks?" Trixie asked as she rubbed her hands together, "It feels like it just ended."

"It ended eight months ago."

Trixie stared at her friend with a frown, "Oh I'm sorry, has my excitement gotten in the way of your realism?"

"I'm just reminding you that the Season ended ages ago."

"You are the weirdest thing . . . You are an author obsessed with facts."

Kaela tried to defend herself, couldn't, gave up and cried, "So the Season starts soon. Who is competing from Apley?"

Trixie smiled and counted off on her fingers, "Angela - naturally. Probably the rest of the advanced class."

"Warren?"

Trixie waited for the flutter of butterflies in her stomach that came at the mention of her crush's name. There were none. She shrugged. Oh well, she'd just have to find a new crush.

"Probably Warren. Bart said he would. From our class is Bella - we are not supporting her."

"Russell will be competing for the first time."

Trixie rolled her eyes at the mention of their friend, "And?"

"It's going to be hard on him. Has he ever competed every second week before?"

Trixie shrugged, "I don't know, Kae, I don't give a special amount of attention to Russell."

"Maybe you should," Kaela said softly and looked at worlds only she could see just outside the window.

Trixie felt her mobile vibrate and dug in her blazer pocket to find it.

"No. No. No!" she cried as she read the text from her sister, Melody.

"What happened?" Kaela asked.

"It's Ronin! He is moving to India! No!"

Kaela was about to ask who Ronin was, but the chaos Trixie's announcement caused on the bus made her think she didn't want to know after all.

"Ronin's moving?" the girl in front asked.

"Our Ronin?" another girl cried.

Within minutes the entire bus of schoolgirls began chatting loudly about Ronin.

"How do you know, Trix?" one of the popular girls cried.

Until that moment, Trixie hadn't been aware that this girl knew her name.

"My sister has been going through all the blog pages about

the show and she said she has read it on a few pages."

As one, the girls (with the exception of Kaela) groaned. Trixie turned back to her mobile and re-read her sister's text.

Kaela rolled her eyes, "You don't think you are getting a little bit too obsessed with that T.V show?"

"He can't go," Trixie whined and completely ignored Kaela's question, "How will he and Isabel get together?"

"You think maybe the writers don't want to get them together?"

"Why?" Trixie wailed.

Kaela shrugged, "To torture the viewers?"

Trixie looked at her in horror, "The writers love us. That's why they have written such a brilliant show for us. That's why they have created such amazing characters and such a beautiful love story. Because they love us."

"And their pay cheques have nothing to do with it?"

Trixie spun on her, "I'll have you know that The Wild Homeopaths is a brilliant show. You should give it a watch sometime."

"I did, and my wild homeopath father says that the show isn't realistic at all. Sending your lead male to India is probably the most truthful thing about homeopathy in that show."

Trixie looked at her in sorrow, "But how will he and Isabel get together now?"

Coming soon in the series...

Book Four

ISBN: 978-1-78226-280-0

Book Five

ISBN: 978-1-78226-281-7

Book Six

ISBN: 978-1-78226-282-4

Pre-order yours today!